Emma's Engagement

Center Point
Large Print

Also by Susan G Mathis and available from Center Point Large Print:

Libby's Lighthouse
Julia's Joy

Emma's Engagement

LOVE AT A LIGHTHOUSE BOOK THREE

SUSAN G MATHIS

CENTER POINT LARGE PRINT
THORNDIKE, MAINE

This Center Point Large Print edition
is published in the year 2025 by arrangement with
Wild Heart Books.

Copyright © 2024 by Susan G Mathis.

All rights reserved.

The characters and events in this fictional work are the product of the author's imagination. Any resemblance to actual people, living or dead, is coincidental.
Unless otherwise indicated, all Scripture quotations are taken from the Holy Bible, King James Version.

The text of this Large Print edition is unabridged.
In other aspects, this book may vary
from the original edition.
Printed in the United States of America
on permanent paper sourced using
environmentally responsible foresting methods.
Set in 16-point Times New Roman type.

ISBN: 979-8-89164-533-2

The Library of Congress has cataloged this record under Library of Congress Control Number: 2025930450

Emma's Engagement

Dedication

To my precious friend, Laurie, who has walked with me through all my stories and became a part of this one. She's toured the Thousand Islands with me and read every word I've written. I still visit the lighthouse every summer.

To the Thousand Islands River Rats and my faithful readers who love the river as much as I do.
Thanks for your support in reading my stories, sharing them with others, and writing reviews.
You bless me.

Chapter 1

Under the warm embrace of the noonday sun, Emma Row grinned at the captivating view—and the handsome lightkeeper standing before her. For the first time, Michael Diepolder had made her a picnic luncheon set on a grassy Thousand Island Park riverbank overlooking Rock Island Lighthouse and the majestic St. Lawrence River. The gentle breeze carried the sweet scent of wildflowers, and the pleasant laughter of river waves provided a melodic backdrop to their intimate alfresco luncheon.

"Oh Michael! It's lovely. Thank you for this."

He reached out and kissed her hand before motioning for her to sit. "You're welcome, dearest. In our three months of courting, you've made all our meals."

"But you've also taken me to the Columbian Hotel for luncheon a dozen times and made me feel more cherished than I could've imagined. I'd almost given up on love, thinking I'd remain buried among novels for the rest of my days."

Michael grinned, giving a half nod. "You *are* cherished, my darling. I wanted today to be extra special. Without distractions."

What was he up to? As a spinster in her thirties, she had resigned herself to a solitary life, living in the boarding house and surrounded by the dusty tomes of the Thousand Island Park library where she worked as a librarian. No family to speak of, but lots of friends in the community.

And then Michael swept into her life.

Emma's pulse ticked up a few notches. He'd spread a cozy blanket on the lush green grass surrounded by the sweet scents of nature, a wicker picnic basket awaiting her discovery. The St. Lawrence River sprawled before them, its tranquil waters reflecting the brilliance of the sunny sky. Rock Island Lighthouse, Michael's home across the main channel, stood proudly as if keeping watch over them.

Clad in his Sunday best, Michael exuded a sense of professionalism and quiet dignity. This man had stolen her heart, her dreams, and her sleep for the past three months. What might his dark, well-trimmed beard feel like? She'd itched to touch it and his curly hair too. They gave him a distinguished and polished look.

His piercing brown eyes conveyed a sense of focus and determination, reflecting the responsibility of his position as a lightkeeper. A hint of a smile graced his face, and a few smile lines feathering around his eyes and across his forehead added to his allure, suggesting he had weathered some difficult experiences and overcome.

Emma pulled her gaze away and sat. She adjusted the skirt of her burgundy dress—her favorite ever since Michael had commented on it, noticing the delicate embroidery and puffed sleeves. She motioned toward the wicker basket. "Shall I?"

His affirming nod and soft smile welcomed her to take a peek as he joined her. She unpacked the picnic basket, revealing an assortment of delicious treats—sandwiches, fresh fruit, and a chilled bottle of lemonade. The atmosphere resounded with the promise of a perfect afternoon.

After Michael gave a blessing, he leaned back on an elbow, staring at the wispy clouds above them. "What a glorious day! Just perfect for late June, don't you think?"

She poured two glasses of lemonade and handed him one, but he didn't drink. What was going on? Despite their brief but sweet courtship, he had always enjoyed food and drink with gusto. But today was different. An air of nervous energy surrounded him, his noticeable lack of appetite puzzling.

"Aren't you hungry? This lemonade is delicious."

Michael's forehead creased in apparent forgetfulness of the lunch before him. He took a sip, reached for a sandwich, and took a bite. "It's simple fare, but I wanted to treat you. You've delighted me with your delicious meals far too often."

She shrugged. "This is very thoughtful, Michael. But besides reading, visiting with friends, and attending church activities, cooking is my favorite pastime."

"Well, then, I'm the luckiest lightkeeper around."

"And I enjoy having someone to cook for."

She sensed he wanted to say something important, but she held her tongue. They indulged in the simple pleasures of their feast, exchanging laughter and tender glances. Though she longed to hear his heart, she had learned that he'd reveal his thoughts when he was ready.

But she couldn't help but steal glimpses at the intriguing man. Rock Island Lighthouse had always fascinated her, and now the lightkeeper did too. "Ever since I moved to Thousand Island Park eight years ago, I've enjoyed seeing the lighthouse. There's something mysterious and enchanting about it."

His face lit up. "I'd like you to see it soon, my darling. I've been working on it. Truly. I want it to be in tip-top shape for your visit."

Emma put down her sandwich. Finally! She'd been longing for the opportunity ever since Mr. Wiseman, her elderly friend and mentor, introduced them three months ago.

Michael grinned, taking her hand in his and giving it a squeeze. "I think the lighthouse is much like our love, Emma. Quiet and steady, yet ready to illuminate the darkest of nights."

Our love? She blinked at his confession. This reserved man had only declared his love once, and he'd shown her only a rare smidgen of affection. His German heritage, she'd reasoned.

She nodded, words lost in the surprise of the moment. Would he say more? Oh, how she hoped so!

For several minutes, they savored the beauty of the day. The river, with its gentle ripples and occasional passing boats, added a sense of tranquility. Seagulls circled overhead, their calls blending harmoniously with the other sounds of nature.

Was that all he had to say? Disappointment tugged at her thoughts. *Patience, Emma. Patience.*

When the meal was done and Emma had packed up the basket, they stood and folded the blanket into a neat little square, setting it atop the basket. But then, Michael turned pensive. Something in his demeanor made her tummy tumble and nerves tingle.

He tugged on his right earlobe as he always did when a mixture of nervousness and anticipation danced in his eyes. He took her hand in his free one. After he sighed deeply, a tiny smile finally settled on his lips.

"Emma Roe, I've waited for this moment for what feels like a lifetime. With every passing day, my love for you has grown stronger. Your sweet, gentle nature adds a sense of peace to life. You bring out the best in me and make me feel complete. So, I must ask, will you be my wife and grow old with me?"

Emma's heart took flight and soared on the breeze, and a squeaky little breath escaped her lips. As an old maid past her prime, she'd waited thirty-seven years. How was she to respond?

Tears of joy spilled down her cheeks as she drank in Michael's soulful gaze. She took a deep breath to steady her nerves. "There's something I need to tell you." Her voice quivered with vulnerability. "Before I met you, I was engaged to a man named Samuel. He was my boss at the milliner's shop, and I thought we had a future together."

Michael listened attentively but said nothing, his face etched with concern.

"But Samuel shattered my heart. He married another hat maker, someone he had known for years. I was devastated, betrayed, and humiliated."

Tears welled up in her eyes as she relived the agonizing memories. She had carried the weight of the man's rejection for years, silently nursing the wounds inflicted by his betrayal.

Michael reached out and gently held her hand, offering her love and reassurance. "My love, I'm so sorry that you had to endure such heartbreak. But please know that you are safe in my arms. I will be here for you. Always."

She bit her lip, holding her breath. Could it be true?

An exasperated expression burst through his grin. "Well?"

"Oh, Michael. I've dreamed of this moment, too, and I can't think of anything I want to do more than spend the rest of my life with you." She threw her arms around him but quickly drew back, surprised at her own gregarious exuberance.

Very unladylike.

Instead of scolding her, he tenderly wiped away her tears and cradled her face in his hands, his eyes fixed upon hers with passion that spoke volumes. Her heart raced with the anticipation of their first kiss, and she met his gaze with an equal measure of affection.

With the sun sprinkling its radiant light upon them, Michael leaned in, closing the distance between them. Their lips met in a sweet, tender kiss, a silent exchange of promises and emotions that needed no words.

The world around them seemed to fade away as they enjoyed the moment. The soft rustle of leaves in the breeze, the distant sounds of the river, and the occasional call of seagulls became mere whispers in the background. All that existed was the warmth of their connection and the joy of their love.

As her fingers gently traced the contours of his hand as they kissed, she felt his pulse that echoed the same rhythm as her own. She'd never been kissed before, not even by Samuel, and the experience felt like a tiny fragment of eternity, a timeless exchange that sealed the commitment of their love.

Captivated by the reality of their engagement, she tugged him closer, cherishing the moment. When they parted, a mutual smile played on their lips, conveying more than words ever could.

Michael touched the tip of her nose. "I love you, my future wife."

Emma giggled. "I love you too."

He pulled her into another warm embrace, and as he held her, Emma dreamed of their future together, their hearts beating in harmony with the rhythm of the river and the promise of many more kisses in the days and years to come.

But Michael was a forty-two-year-old widower and father to Ada. He knew the intimacies of marriage and family. She did not. And his eleven-year-old daughter would likely bring blessings—and challenges—to their union. Could she live up to his expectations of being a wife and mother?

When she looked into his eyes, Michael gifted her with a gaze that spoke of the future. Perhaps she could do it. She'd give it her best.

As she basked in the joy of their engagement, he guided her to a cozy bench nearby where they could sit together, still overlooking the river and the distant lighthouse.

The lighthouse would one day be her home! She let out a hearty laugh as her excitement overflowed. "I've always wondered what it would be like to live on a tiny island, but to live in a lighthouse? I never imagined I'd have such a blessing. I also suspect it'll be, well, different, to be a lightkeeper's wife—with the long hours, isolation, and the duties—but I'll do my best. I'm sure it will be quite a change from my life as a librarian here in Thousand Island Park."

He sighed, compassion shining in his eyes. "I hate that you'd have to give up your work for me, and I know it won't be easy, my love. But together, every challenge will be an adventure."

As they continued to gaze at the lighthouse, Emma pondered the sacrifices she'd make—especially leaving behind her role as a librarian and her connections to the tight-knit Thousand Island Park community. Yet the prospect of building a life with Michael filled her with a sense of unparalleled happiness.

With a tender smile, she whispered, "I'll gladly give it up for you, Michael. Being your wife will surely be the greatest adventure I could ever imagine."

Michael sucked in a steadying breath as he held his soon-to-be bride close, the gentle librarian who charmed everyone frequenting the Park's library. Her shy nature made her approachable and inviting for those seeking assistance among the bookshelves. She was always ready to provide a listening ear to those in need. Behind her reading spectacles, her warm mahogany eyes held a depth of knowledge and empathy. Despite her gentle disposition, she also harbored a curious strength, probably from the debacle with that rogue, Samuel . . . and with so many years of being on her own. When faced with challenges, Emma exhibited resilience and determination, just what she'd need to be a lightkeeper's wife and a step-mother. Best of all, her love for literature and the pursuit of knowledge made her all the more interesting. That'd be welcome on those long winter nights. He'd come to love her for all of it.

How someone hadn't won her heart before now was a mystery and a gift.

Somehow, in God's great mercy, *he* had won her heart! He wanted to jump up from that bench and shout it to the world. Instead, he sat next to her, quietly thanking the good Lord for her.

Michael dipped his chin. "Do you think some of your family might join us for the wedding? My parents can no longer travel, so we'll have no family here if they don't."

Emma frowned. "I'm afraid none of my family will attend. As you know, I was one of seven siblings—three sisters and three brothers. But over the years, our family has fallen apart after our parents passed away. My father succumbed to an illness, and my mother followed soon after. My eldest sister got married and moved away, and we've grown distant over the years. One of my sisters has been gone for decades and the other one died in a carriage accident."

Michael took her hand and patted it gently. "I'm so sorry, Emma."

She shrugged, a deep sigh punctuating her sadness. "My brothers have busy lives, and I've lost touch with them too. My heart aches for the close-knit group we once were. So no, I'm afraid none of my family will be able to join us on our special day. It will just be us and the Thousand Islands community who loves us."

Would the pain Emma had endured help her handle the challenges that awaited her on tiny Rock Island—and the isolation? She'd voiced her apprehensions, valid ones he shared, about the responsibilities of being a lightkeeper's wife. But she hadn't mentioned her role as a stepmother to his eleven-year-old daughter, Ada. That worried him the most.

Though he should discuss the matter with her, he hesitated. He had wanted to savor this perfect moment, to bask in the joy of their love before broaching the topic.

He shifted to face Emma, who stared at the lighthouse across the water. The sparkle in her eyes mirrored the radiance of the sun, and for a moment, Michael found himself captivated by the beauty of the scene and the woman beside him.

Her thin, narrow face, tiny turned-up nose, and full pink lips reminded him so much of Ada. So did her thick auburn hair. Why, they could pass for mother and daughter.

But how would Emma feel about that? How would Ada?

Could Emma be happy with life on the tiny island, the duties of being a lightkeeper's wife, *and* her role as stepmother? Though they'd talked about Ada several times, Emma had yet to meet her.

During the school year, Ada lived in Rochester, New York, over a hundred and fifty miles away. She stayed with his mother, her beloved granny, and he rarely got to see her, save at Christmas, when he traveled there. Now she'd be home for the summer, just as she had for the past four years.

He took a deep breath, searching for the right words. "There's something I need to talk to you about." He rubbed his earlobe as his gaze shifted to a passing boat before returning to face her.

Emma's expression turned from curiosity to concern. "What is it, Michael?"

"My daughter, Ada, is coming home. In two days." He told her about a telegram he'd received announcing Ada's return and how he looked forward to having her around.

A range of emotions played across Emma's face—curiosity, apprehension, and perhaps a touch of nervousness. The initial joy of their perfect day was tempered by the reality of responsibilities and adjustments they'd soon have to face.

Emma swallowed, a small smile quivering on her lips. "I look forward to meeting her, Michael. You've told me a little about her, but tell me more. Please. I want to know everything."

"Well, Ada loves drawing and science, especially astronomy. She's smart, curious . . . and a bit tenacious. In all honesty, this marriage might be quite an adjustment for her, as it may for you. Still, I'm sure you'll make a great mother, Emma, and we'll face every challenge together."

Emma nodded, listening attentively, her hands clasped together in her lap. When he finished, a moment of silence set his nerves on edge.

Suddenly, Emma leaned over and kissed his cheek. That unspoken agreement to face whatever lay ahead sent a wave of relief and gratitude over him.

Understanding and determination sparked in her eyes. "I'm sure I'll love her as much as I love her father." Emma slipped her arm into the crook of his and squeezed it. She laid her head on his shoulder. "Does she remember her mother?"

His pulse quickened at her nearness. Soon they could share many such moments together. "Yes. Ada and my late wife were like two peas in a pod.

They shared an incredible bond that was evident in everything they did together."

"That's how my mother and I were, too, even though I had six siblings."

His gaze wandered to the lighthouse. "Her mother died when she was seven, before I took the post of lightkeeper, but even these four years later, Ada still misses her terribly. Losing her at such a young age has left lasting scars on her, so I'm uneasy about how she'll accept you. I've mentioned you in my letters to her, but . . ."

Emma patted his hand. "I'm sure it'll be fine, Michael, but I'm sorry for her loss—and yours."

"Ada is a beautiful and smart girl, Emma. She has this way of looking at the world that just captivates you. But she also lacks a bit of self-confidence, probably from the loss. It can sometimes come across as a little obstinate, but deep down, I think it's her way of coping. I hope she doesn't give you trouble."

For several long moments, Emma said nothing. Was he scaring her? Would she renege on the betrothal?

His heart held a tinge of remorse that lingered just beneath the surface. If he were honest, he doted on Ada far too much. But their bond was undeniable, a connection that transcended the physical distance that separated them every school year.

He loved his daughter more than his own life.

How would Emma fit into that closeness without straining it?

His mind journeyed back to the day he had accepted the position of lightkeeper, just months after his wife's tragic passing. But the responsibility of the job required his full attention, leaving him with a difficult decision—how to ensure Ada's well-being and education. Unable to juggle both roles effectively—and the depth of their grief—he made the heart-wrenching decision to send her to live with his mother in Rochester.

From that day since, guilt had settled in his chest like an anchor, a constant reminder of the sacrifice he had made for the sake of his duty. He had wanted the best for Ada, but the decision, while practical, oppressed him. The distance between them had only intensified the longing, and regret lingered in the corners of his mind.

As Michael sat next to Emma surrounded by the rhythmic waves of the river, he replayed moments from Ada's childhood in his memory. Her laughter, the way her eyes danced with curiosity, and the warmth of her hugs flooded his thoughts.

A sigh escaped his lips, a mixture of love and remorse. If only he could turn back time—find a way to be both the father she deserved and the lightkeeper the river community depended upon. Remorse might linger, but so did the determination to be the father Ada deserved, especially this summer. Emma could play an important part in it all.

Emma interrupted his musings. "I'm not worried, Michael. Every child has his or her challenges. We'll face Ada's together."

He blew out a deep breath, his thoughts reflecting a complexity of emotions. "You're a gift from God, Emma. Ada is at that age where she needs a mother, but she can be impulsive and stubborn. It's part of growing pains, I suppose. But, underneath it all, she has a heart as big as this river."

Emma shifted in her seat. "I'm sure she does. You said she enjoys drawing and science. What else does she like?"

A warm chuckle escaped him. "We go fishing together pretty often. She often drags me from the tower for a quiet morning on the water. And at night, she loves to join me on the parapet to stare at the constellations. It's our way of connecting since we lost her mother."

"That sounds lovely. Peaceful." Did her tone hold a trace of doubt about how she would fit in?

His eyes met Emma's, gratitude and affection filling his heart. "Though Ada may be tough on the outside, she's still a little girl yearning for love and understanding. I believe together we can offer her that, Emma. I believe you can be the anchor both of us need."

"I'd be honored, Michael, and I'll do my best."

While the decision to marry had been made in the quiet corners of his heart, now that it was real, he couldn't imagine facing the upcoming chapter without Emma by his side.

His pulse quickened as a new possibility dawned. "My sweet Emma. What would you think if we were to marry right away so we can enjoy the summer as a family?"

Chapter 2

Three days later, Emma scurried to the Thousand Island Park dock, a few minutes late after a library patron kept her too long. She was greeted by the rhythmic creaking of the boats against the wooden moorings, and one of them was Michael's.

His face lit up with a welcoming smile as he waved hello and gestured toward Ada. The gentle ripples played with the boat while Michael stood proudly by his St. Lawrence skiff, his eleven-year-old daughter beside him, her demeanor giving away little about her thoughts.

He bowed slightly, grinning widely. "Good morning, Emma. I'd like you to meet Ada."

Ada's eyes, rich with silver hues, held a spark that alternated between a warmth reminiscent of her father's and a hint of hostility, serving as a silent warning to Emma. Her thick brown hair held shades of auburn so much like Emma's own. Despite her age, Ada was thin and small. But the girl's exceptional beauty surpassed her years, making her the loveliest child Emma had ever laid eyes on.

When she flashed a smile at her father, huge dimples in her thin but pretty face added charm to her countenance. But when she sized up Emma, her pursed lips and knit brows displayed subtle disapproval. A twinge of uncertainty sent a shiver up Emma's spine.

"Hello, Ada." Emma greeted her with the most pleasant tone she could muster, attempting to break through the wall of disapproval. "It's so good to finally meet you. Your father just adores you and has told me so much about you."

Emma put out her hand, but Ada offered only a curt nod. With introductions made, Michael helped them into the skiff, and once they settled, they set off to cross the narrow channel on the short trip to Rock Island.

The boat sliced through the water, carrying an unspoken tension. Emma stole glances at Ada. What thoughts lay hidden behind her pursed lips and narrowed eyes?

Michael attempted to break the silence. "I'm glad you two finally met. I hope you'll be best of friends by and by."

Emma let out a puff of air. "I'm sure we will, won't we, Ada?"

The girl shrugged, and when Michael turned his attention to rowing out into the channel, Ada cast her a wary scowl. Emma could almost hear Ada's teeth grinding in challenge. Her stomach constricted. And just when she thought she'd have a perfect little family in her life.

As the skiff moved across the channel, sunlight danced on the waves, casting reflections that mirrored the complexities between the three of them. The journey to Rock Island held a silent, mysterious undercurrent, leaving Emma with a boatload of apprehension.

In the distance, a colossal ship came into view, its silhouette imposing against the horizon. Captivated by the sheer size of the vessel, Emma exchanged wide-eyed glances with Ada. A marvel of maritime engineering, the ship moved gracefully through the water, leaving a trail of frothy waves in its wake.

Though Emma had been on the river with these giant vessels before, it always delighted her. Unfazed by the river traffic, Michael skillfully maneuvered the skiff as the ship drew closer. When the two boats crossed paths, sailors on the larger vessel waved enthusiastically in their direction. Emma waved back, and Ada did, too, caught in a moment of mutual awe. The sailors' distant shouts of greeting carried across the water, adding a friendly touch to the encounter.

"Look at the size of that ship, Ada," Emma exclaimed, her voice carrying a hint of amazement.

Ada's smile momentarily broke the guarded expression she had maintained. But then, she waved a hand dismissively before shifting her body away from Emma. "I've seen lots of them up close."

Michael's gaze darted between Emma and

his daughter, but he said nothing. Indeed, he remained silent as the towering masts and billowing sails dwarfed everything in its wake. While the ship continued its journey, disappearing into the horizon, the skiff pressed on toward the quiet sanctuary of Rock Island.

Emma prayed that even that tiny shared awe-filled moment with Ada would break the icy waters between them. But when Ada folded her arms and glared at her, Emma wondered if this marriage was a good idea or a fool's undertaking.

Once they crossed the channel and approached Rock Island, Emma viewed the island up close for the first time, the place that was to become her home soon. Goodbye to the noisy boarding house. Hello to this quiet, isolated island.

The large, well-kept, one-and-a-half story, shingle-style Victorian stood in the middle of the island, facing north toward Thousand Island Park, surrounded by a concrete seawall for protection.

"Why, the cottage is bigger than my boarding house," Emma exclaimed. It must have ten rooms or more. "That's why the lighthouse is so hard to see. How strange." She pointed to the left a few yards from the cottage. "Why didn't they build the light on the shore?"

Michael leaned closer. "It's a strange placement, to be sure. The conical iron tower was erected on the bedrock at the center of the island, about fifteen feet above the river, on the highest point on the island. That makes it a sturdy light, but it also obscures its view. Still, it's forty-five feet high and holds a sixth-order Fresnel lens."

Emma furrowed her brow. "Even from the Park it can be hard to see, especially painted brown and set back so far."

Michael nodded. "Indeed. I urged the lighthouse board to consider moving the light to the edge of the shore, but they're yet to implement my request. Perhaps one day. Until then, I must keep a vigilant eye out. After the tower was erected at the center of the island, shipwrecks in the vicinity increased because the house, trees, and other lights from the mainland obscure the ship pilots' perceptions of the beacon."

His irritation evident, she turned the conversation to a lighter topic. "The covered porch must be a wonderful place to sit in the evening and view the ships passing by."

Ada scowled, letting out a tiny groan. "My papa and I like to watch the sunset. Together. Just the two of us."

Michael glanced at his daughter but quickly turned his attention back to Emma, pointing out the other structures on the island. To the east, a carpenter's shop, and behind that, the powerhouse. The tiny fieldstone smokehouse stood just to the right of the cottage, and beyond that, a barn and icehouse. She'd always wondered what those little buildings were, and now she knew.

When they docked the skiff and Michael helped Ada and herself out of the boat, Emma asked, "Do you have a privy or indoor plumbing?"

"The privy is just beyond the light."

Ada huffed, rolling her eyes. "We have indoor plumbing at Granny's and at school. Not like here."

Emma shrugged, trying to ignore the girl's comment. "If you'll excuse me, then, I'll return in a moment."

Michael waved an arm toward a tiny building. "Take your time. Our privy is not the fanciest, but it'll do."

She made her way to the edge of the southern shoreline where she found the beginning of a walkway to a bridge stretching out over the river. Could that tiny building be the privy? For such a large and comely home? It must be, since it was the only structure near where Michael had gestured. Even the boarding house had indoor plumbing, and so did her childhood home. Could she endure such primitive accommodations, especially when the cold winds blew? She shuddered at the thought.

A narrow bridge offered the only path to the outhouse, and the wooden planks creaked under her weight. Perched on stilts and standing about eight feet from the water, the privy looked like a tiny wooden cabin suspended in midair. The outhouse was a humble four-by-four-foot structure with a latched door, adorned with a half-moon cutout.

Amusement tickled a chuckle from her at the unconventional nature of this bathroom. Opening the door with a creak, Emma stepped into the small space. Light through the cutout illuminated the interior, revealing the open water below through the comfort perch. Goodness! How odd. What other strange things might she face in this place?

When she completed her visit, Emma emerged into the bright sunlight, ready to make her way back along the narrow bridge to the cozy cottage and her future there.

But what about the peculiar nature of this child who would soon be her daughter?

The warm breeze brushed against Michael's face as he stood at the cottage door waiting for Emma's return, his heart heavy with love and disquiet. Ada stood nearby, her arms crossed defiantly over her chest. Her eyes, usually bright with joy, now clouded with anger and hurt.

"Come on, Ada." He reached out to give her a quick hug. "We've talked about this. You know Emma means a lot to me, and we are getting married. Tomorrow. You'll be our flower girl and wear the pretty pink dress I bought for you. Please try to be a little nicer to her."

Ada shrugged away from his touch, her resentment palpable. "I don't want her here, and I don't want you to marry. She's going to ruin everything, and I don't need a stepmother."

His heart sank at her words, his own pain mingling with hers. He had hoped this would be easier. "Ada, sweetheart, Emma is not trying to replace your mother. She just wants to be a part of our lives."

But Ada wasn't listening. Her shoulders slumped, and she turned away, her steps heavy as she retreated to her room, leaving him standing alone, his heart aching with the weight of her rejection. What was he going to do?

He wanted to go after her, to comfort her, to reassure her that everything would be okay. But he'd failed her again. Seemed that no matter how hard he tried, he couldn't be the father she needed, let alone the mother she yearned for.

Yet Ada was so much like him that he knew she needed time to process her feelings, to come to terms with the changes in their lives. Perhaps she'd come around sooner rather than later?

With a heavy sigh, he made his way toward the lighthouse. When she returned from the privy, he'd show Emma the tower's inner workings—and the incredible view. But even as he waited to show her the light for the first time and observe her face light up with wonder, his thoughts were of Ada, his beloved daughter whose pain he couldn't bear to witness. Her words echoed in his mind.

Her resistance to Emma's presence and her fear of change haunted him.

Yes, he understood Ada's apprehension, her angst over losing the life they had built together. Ever since his wife passed away, they had formed a bond that was unbreakable even with distance, a bond born out of shared grief and unwavering love.

But he also couldn't deny the love he felt for Emma, the way she had brought light back into his life after years of darkness. Emma empathized with his pain, his loss, in a way that no one else had, and no matter how much Ada objected, he couldn't let Emma go.

Was he being selfish, putting his own happiness above his daughter's? Was he asking too much of her, expecting her to accept Emma into their lives without question?

He didn't have all the answers, didn't know how to reassure her that everything would work out. But he knew that he had to try, for her sake, for Emma's sake, for the sake of the love that bound them together, even in the face of uncertainty.

When Emma joined him at the lighthouse tower, her soft lavender dress accentuating her slim figure, Michael couldn't help but admire his bride-to-be, his heart swelling with anticipation. He couldn't wait to share the beauty of the lighthouse and the breathtaking view from the top.

"Are you ready?" He reached out to take her hand.

She nodded, her eyes shining with curiosity and wonder. "I can't wait to see it. I've dreamed of climbing to the top ever since I first saw it."

His pulse quickened as he led her up the narrow, winding staircase, each metal step bringing them closer to the top. They climbed higher and higher, the air cooling and the squawking of the circling gulls growing louder.

Finally, they reached the top and stepped out onto the parapet that encircled the light room. Emma drew in a deep breath in awe, as he knew she would. She took in the panoramic view, the vast expanse of the river stretching before them. He delighted at her childlike wonder as she pointed to Thousand Island Park across the channel and giggled.

"Seeing the Park from this perch is wonderful, Michael, and this view is even more beautiful than I'd imagined." Her eyes sparkled, and her voice resounded with joy.

His heart swelled with pride as she took in the view. "I wanted to show you the beauty of this place before we wed. It mirrors the beauty of our love, I think."

Emma's eyes brimmed with tears as she turned to him. Without a word, she wrapped her arms around him, holding him close as they stood together on top of the world, their love shining brighter than the beacon of the lighthouse itself.

He brushed a kiss on the top of her head. "Emma, I'm sorry for Ada's cold reception earlier. She's just . . . struggling with the idea of us being together."

She gently squeezed him, but when she pulled back, her eyes were filled with compassion. "It's okay, Michael. I understand this is a big adjustment for her. She's been through so much already, losing her mother, attending school so far from you, and now facing the prospect of a stepmother."

He sighed, grateful for her understanding. "I just worry that I'm asking too much of her, expecting her to accept you into our lives without any reservations. And asking too much of you too."

Emma's smile held warmth and reassurance. "You're not asking too much, Michael. Ada loves you, and she'll come around in her own time. All we can do is be patient and give her the space she needs to adjust. But perhaps . . . maybe we should postpone the wedding until the end of summer?"

What? No! He tensed at her suggestion. He shook his head. "No, my love. I feel strongly that we must show her we are a family as we journey through this summer together. Yet I fear it may be fraught with stormy seas. Are you prepared for that?"

She ran her hand across his beard, her touch sending a shiver of warmth coursing through him. "Then we'll show her and tackle the storms together. I believe in us, and I believe in Ada. We'll find a way to make this work."

He kissed her on the forehead. "Are you ready to wed tomorrow, then?"

She nodded, a sweet giggle revealing her happiness. "I'm so ready, Michael! The church is booked, and the wedding breakfast is planned for the Columbian. Mr. Wiseman will be our officiant. And don't you worry. I'll win the heart of your girl if it's the last thing I do."

"Thank you for that." He took her hand. "Let's go and have lunch with our Ada before I take you home to prepare for our special day."

Emma squeezed his hand. "Our Ada? I like the sound of that."

When they entered the cottage, Emma helped him set out sandwiches, pickled beets, and bowls of fresh berries. Sunlight streamed through the windows of the cozy kitchen as the three of them sat down for lunch, but the atmosphere was tense.

As they ate, Emma regaled them with stories of her time as a librarian, her face lighting up with enthusiasm as she spoke about her love of books and learning. But Ada's mood remained somber, her gaze fixed on her plate as she pushed her food around with her fork.

He handed Ada a bowl of berries, bidding her to enter the conversation. "What's on your mind, sweetheart?"

A shadow fell across her face, her expression growing stormy as she hesitated to speak. Finally, she took a deep breath. "Librarians are awful. Mrs. Crenshaw is the librarian at my school, but she's as mean as a barnyard dog."

Emma tilted her head, her brows furrowing. "What do you mean?"

Ada's eyes narrowed as she trained them on Emma. "Librarians hate children. Mrs. Crenshaw growls and scolds us incessantly for the smallest things, like talking too loudly or not returning our books on time. She even rapped me on the knuckles with her ruler once. She makes us feel as though we're not welcome in the library, as though we're nothing but a nuisance to her. I hate her."

His fists clenched at the thought of someone mistreating his daughter, his protective instincts on full alert. "I'm sorry you went through that, Ada. No one deserves to be treated that way, especially not by someone who's supposed to be helping them learn and grow. But all librarians don't hate children, and we don't hate people. Not anyone. Not even her."

Emma nodded. "That's true. I promise, I'm not like that. You should never have to feel afraid or unwelcome at school. The library should be a wonderful, safe space you can learn and explore."

"I don't need a mother!" Ada slammed her hands on the table, her voice rising. "Especially a librarian!" Her words echoed off the walls of the cottage.

Michael's emotions swirled with anger, guilt, and sorrow. Anger at that Crenshaw woman. Guilt that he sent his daughter to that school. Sorrow that Ada was hurt. But he was even more saddened by the outburst and all that lay underneath it. He had hoped that lunch together would bring them closer as a family, but now he feared that he had only succeeded in driving them further apart.

Emma scooted her chair closer and gently placed her hand on Ada's shoulder, her touch a loving gesture amid the tension that hung in the air. "Ada, I'm not like Mrs. Crenshaw, nor am I trying to replace your mother. I just want to be a part of your life, to love you and support you in any way that I can."

Emma's eyes and voice were filled with so much empathy, it brought tears to his eyes. How could he be so blessed to have such a woman want to marry him?

Ada's shoulders sagged, her anger visibly melting away as she looked up at Emma with a remorseful gaze.

Emma smiled softly. "It's okay, Ada. We'll figure this out together, as a family."

But could they become a family, or would life be rife with tension from now on?

Chapter 3

Emma stood inside the quaint Thousand Island Park church vestibule, her heart pounding with anticipation as she peeked through the sanctuary door. Sunlight streamed through the stained-glass windows, casting colorful patterns on the polished wooden pews. Wildflowers adorned the altar. The guests waited . . . for her.

She closed the door and whispered a prayer of gratitude. "Thank you, God, for this day!" But a small piece of her ached for the disenfranchised family she wished were here.

Nervous energy coursed through her veins, both excitement and apprehension swirling within her. At long last. The day she would marry the man of her dreams and embark on a new chapter of their lives together. Tonight, they would stay at the Columbian as husband and wife. Tomorrow, they would begin their journey as a family, living in the picturesque lighthouse on Rock Island. It all seemed too good to be true.

As she stood at the threshold of her new life, the weight of her impending role as a stepmother tainted her joy, just a little. She took a deep breath, trying to quell the fluttering in her stomach, but the nervous anticipation churned within her. The thought of stepping into such a significant role, of taking on the responsibility of caring for young Ada, filled her with both excitement and trepidation.

With determination burning in her heart, Emma made a silent vow to herself. She would give it her all, pouring every ounce of love and devotion into her new roles as wife and mother. She would stand by Ada, support her, and guide her through life's ups and downs, just as she would if she had her own child.

She closed her eyes and whispered a silent prayer, asking the Almighty for strength, for wisdom, and for the ability to make a positive difference in the child's life. She prayed that she would be able to nurture the girl, to help her flourish and grow into the remarkable person she was destined to become.

Ada entered the vestibule and joined her, a large bouquet of peonies in one hand and a basket of wildflowers in the other. She nodded to Emma, a wide smile and huge dimples enhancing her pretty face.

Perhaps the winds of animosity had blown over.

"Oh, Ada! You look lovely. That pink dress suits you."

Ada thrust the bouquet toward Emma, a mischievous glint in her eye. The child's grin widened as Emma accepted the flowers.

Such a sweet and thoughtful gesture. Emma's

heart swelled with love for her soon-to-be stepdaughter.

But as her fingers brushed against the delicate petals, her warm sentiments shifted from joy to confusion, then horror. A shiver ran down her spine as she felt something crawling on her skin. With a gasp, she recoiled, dropping the bouquet to the ground. Peonies scattered in all directions as she frantically brushed little black dots from her cream-colored gown, surprise and disgust welling up inside her.

"What . . . what's happening?" Emma's voice trembled with disbelief. What had the girl done?

Ada burst into laughter and doubled over, clutching her stomach as tears of mirth streamed down her cheeks.

"It's . . . it's full of ants!" Anger and embarrassment flushed Emma's cheeks red hot. Why would the girl do such a thing?

Amid Ada's laughter, Emma's indignation slowly melted. She glanced down at the scattered peonies and fleeing ants, and a smile tugged at the corners of her lips. A childish prank?

No harm done. But she'd not let the girl get the best of her. No way!

"You little rascal!" Emma teased, forcing her tone to sound affectionate as she reached out to tousle Ada's hair.

Ada stepped back to avoid contact. She feigned innocence. "I thought you might need some extra company on your walk down the aisle, Emma."

"So you knew I was nervous about walking down the aisle alone?" Emma spread a smile on her face. "How thoughtful of you."

Ada's mouth dropped open and she spluttered a moment, until Emma gave her a nudge toward the sanctuary door. "Head on down the aisle, Ada. Your father is waiting for us."

Ada shot her a mysterious glance, causing Emma to hesitate. The enigma of the girl could wait. There were more important matters at hand.

Emma left the peonies—and the ants—scattered on the floor. She folded her hands, and with a steadying breath, she stepped into the church, her heart swelling with hope.

At the ripe old age of thirty-seven, she could hardly believe that this day had finally come—the day she had dreamed of since she was a little girl. As she took her first steps down the aisle, her eyes fixed on the altar where Michael stood waiting for her, a sense of peace washed over her.

The soft strains of the organ filled the air, and the congregation stood to watch her. Ada, in her pretty pink dress, was already halfway down the aisle, dramatically scattering wildflowers that matched those on the altar.

Emma's heart raced as she caught Michael's eager gaze. He offered her a reassuring smile, his eyes filled with love and devotion. Her smile blossomed so wide, it almost hurt.

When she reached his side, they exchanged a tender glance, and their hands found each other's in a silent promise.

Michael leaned in and whispered, "Good morning, my love."

"Good morning, Michael." Emma smiled at her soon-to-be husband, but out of the corner of her eye, she caught Ada's as the girl sat in the front pew casting her a narrow-eyed scowl.

Pastor Wiseman, their elderly friend who had matched them up, began the ceremony, his voice echoing through the hallowed halls. "Dearly beloved, we are gathered here today to witness and celebrate the union of Emma Row and Michael Diepolder in holy matrimony."

She listened attentively, for she wanted to remember every moment of this day. Amid the solemnity, a sense of joy and expectancy filled her heart.

"Marriage is a sacred covenant, a union not to be entered into lightly, but with reverence and respect. Emma and Michael, as you stand here today, may your love continue to grow and flourish, may you support and cherish one another through all the joys and challenges that life may bring, and may God lead the way."

Pastor Wiseman continued the ceremony, speaking of love, commitment, and the sacred bond of marriage. Surrounded by their loved ones, they recited their vows, their words carrying a lifetime of promises. With each "I do," Emma's anxiety about Ada melted away, replaced by a sense of joy and celebration.

Finally, with a triumphant flourish, the pastor pronounced them husband and wife. The church erupted into applause as they enjoyed their first kiss as a married couple, sealing their union with a tender embrace.

They turned to face their guests, and a sea of smiling faces and outstretched hands awaited them—save Ada, who sat pouting, her arms folded and head down. Michael momentarily left Emma's side, took his daughter's hand, and tugged her to join them. She followed, but a scowl kept her dimples hidden.

Together, the three of them walked down the aisle, hand in hand, ready to embark on the adventure of marriage and family—a journey that Emma trusted would be filled with love, challenges, and countless blessings to come. No matter what lay ahead, she and Michael would face it together, guided by their love and faith.

After they stepped outside the church into a warm summer morning, their guests gathered around them, offering heartfelt well-wishes and promises of support as they congratulated them as newlyweds. Smiles graced the faces of friends and family, their joy palpable.

Perhaps Ada would catch a bit of that enthusiasm.

Michael beamed with obvious pride as he looked at both her and Ada, each clinging to one of his arms. "Well, family." His voice was filled with warmth and affection. "Shall we stroll to the Columbian to enjoy our wedding breakfast?"

Ada's response shattered the moment like fragile glass. "I'm not hungry. I don't want to go and celebrate. I hate this day."

Emma's heart sank as she assessed Ada, the child's eyes brimming with tears. A pang of guilt washed over her, for the child would likely be struggling with the idea of their new family dynamic for some time to come. Indeed, she might always struggle with it. At the very least, this could be a long, hard summer.

Michael's smile faltered, replaced by a long stare of concern and compassion. He gently patted his daughter's shoulder. "Ada, sweetheart, I understand that today may be difficult for you. But it'd be easier on all of us if you'd celebrate with us. We love you, and we'll work together to make this transition as easy as possible."

Emma nodded, her cheeks growing warm at the public slight, her heart aching for Ada's pain—and her own. Would everyone notice that Ada didn't like her and judge her as an unfit stepmother? Would Michael regret he'd married her?

As they turned to walk to the hotel and face the road ahead, she whispered a silent prayer for healing and harmony in the days to come and that their love would be their guiding light, illuminating the path toward a brighter tomorrow.

But the question remained—would Ada allow the light to shine?

Inside the stately Columbian Hotel adorned with cascading blooms and delicate lace, guests mingled in the opulent dining room. The sun cast a warm glow over the elegant breakfast gathering, where Michael and his bride took their places of honor at a table adorned with crisp linens and delicate china. Despite the laughter, lively chatter, and clinking of glasses around him, Michael's mind fixed on Ada. Worry marred his joy as he watched her join friends across the room.

Ada sat with Stella Everson and Maude Armstrong, elderly aunts to young Mary Flynn with whom she would be spending the night. He'd hoped his daughter would be happy to be with a playmate, but perhaps he was wrong. Perhaps he'd miscalculated the depth of her resistance to the marriage.

Ada's usually cheerful demeanor seemed overshadowed by a veil of resentment. Her gaze was fixed on her plate, her fork waving in the air aimlessly.

He patted Emma's hand. "If you'll excuse me

for a moment, my darling. I think our girl needs a bit of tender loving care."

She nodded, an encouraging smile bolstering him. "Of course, Michael."

Driven by the haunting pang of guilt, he made his way over to Ada. As he approached, a frown tugged at the corners of her lips.

"Hello, my girl." He slid into the seat beside her and nodded greetings to the aunts and Mary. "How are you doing, sweetheart?"

Ada shrugged, avoiding his gaze. "I'm okay, I guess."

His heart sank at the lackluster response. He reached out and brushed her cheek, gentle and reassuring. "I know this isn't easy for you, but your happiness means the world to me. Try to have fun."

She glanced up, her eyes shimmering with unshed tears. She whispered so her tablemates couldn't hear. "I just . . . I don't want things to change, Papa. I'm afraid of losing you."

His heart clenched at her words. He wrapped an arm around her shoulders, pulling her close in a comforting embrace.

"Ada, you'll never lose me. Never." His voice was unwavering with conviction. "You will always be my girl, no matter what. Emma is not here to replace anyone. She's here to join our family and share in our love."

Ada sniffled, her tears spilling over as she

buried her face against his chest. From now on, he'd have to delicately dance between his two ladies, managing the relationships carefully.

Should he have waited to marry, as Emma had suggested? Too late for that now.

He slipped Ada his handkerchief as her young friend watched intently. "So, Mary, how are you enjoying the summer at Thousand Island Park?"

The eight-year-old's eyes danced. "I love it here. Watertown is far too hot in the summer. And my aunties are wonderful."

Stella guffawed. "For a couple of old hens, I guess." The self-proclaimed community gossip and matchmaker had to be twenty pounds heavier than her quiet younger sister, Maude, whose perfectly coifed gray hair displayed her attention to detail.

Maude smiled sweetly. "We just love having Mary with us, and we're happy to have Ada join us anytime she'd like to visit."

Mary nodded. "We'll have so much fun, Ada. You just wait and see."

Michael kissed Ada on the cheek. "She'll enjoy it, I'm sure. But now, I need to go. Duty calls."

Ada pursed her lips but acquiesced. "Bye, Papa." She took a sip of her lemonade without saying more.

Michael joined Emma as she chatted with his friend, John Kuek, and her friend, Nellie Johnston, both impeccably dressed and exuding elegance as they engaged in lively conversation by a sunlit window.

John smiled admiringly. "Miss Johnston, I must say, you look absolutely radiant today."

Nellie's cheeks pinked as she returned the compliment. "Thank you, Mr. Kuek. It's an honor to attend this wonderful wedding. And might I say, you are quite the dapper gentleman yourself."

Emma chuckled. "Nellie is truly radiant. I agree, sir."

John clicked his tongue. "But you, Mrs. Diepolder, are the belle of the ball for sure."

Michael guffawed. "True enough, John, but your habit of flattery will get you into trouble someday. Mark my words."

Emma's best friend, Laurie Jean, and her husband, Robert, joined them. The couples visited for several moments before their guests dispersed into the crowd.

Emma leaned close to him. "How's Ada faring? I'm praying for her. I hope her day isn't spoilt."

He patted her arm. "She'll be fine in time. Let's go and enjoy a treat."

When they neared the pastry table, Ada and her friend were already there, along with Mary's chaperones. Mary eagerly pointed to the array of delectable baked goods. "Aunty Stella, Aunty Maude, may I please have one of those lovely pastries?"

Her aunts smiled indulgently, granting her

permission for both of them to enjoy a treat. Stella turned to him apologetically. "I hope you permit such indulgences?"

He laughed. "Of course. Treat Ada as your own. Whatever she wants is fine with me. Thank you for taking her for the night."

He glanced at Emma, whose face flushed pink. Was she as excited about their wedding night as he?

Mary eagerly reached for an éclair, her giggle interrupting his thoughts of the evening ahead.

Mr. E.F. Otis, the esteemed proprietor of the TI Park bookstore, approached, extending a warm greeting. "Ah, congratulations, Mr. and Mrs. Diepolder. It's a sad day here in the Park for losing our favorite librarian and a good neighbor. I'm not sure I can forgive you for that, Michael." Mr. Otis's dark mustache wiggled as he spoke.

Michael clapped him on the shoulder. "Sorry about that, chap. But your loss is my gain, and remember, she's just across the channel. We'll visit often enough, I assure you."

Otis nodded. "Very good, then. Thanks for inviting me today. This is a smashing party."

Nearby, Mrs. Arthur, proprietor of the Art Needlework Shop, engaged in spirited conversation with Mr. and Mrs. S.C. Judson, celebrated artists renowned for their breathtaking paintings. Emma excused herself to join them, hugging the women and chatting happily. Michael's heart clenched at the thought he was taking Emma away from this close-knit community. How would she handle the isolation away from the people here?

Just then, Mr. Watkin, owner of the local bakery and ice cream pavilion, made a grand entrance carrying a magnificent tiered wedding cake. The guests gasped in awe at the sight of the exquisite creation, their admiration palpable as Emma joined Michael at the cake table.

"Ladies and gentlemen, may I present the pièce de résistance of today's festivities—our splendid wedding cake!" Mr. Watkin set the cake on the table and waved an arm dramatically.

Mr. Lesesne, the local photographer, prepared to immortalize the momentous occasion with his camera. With practiced precision, he adjusted his equipment, ensuring every detail would be captured flawlessly for posterity.

"Stand still, Mr. and Mrs. Diepolder, and let me capture the moment." His tone carried authority and professionalism.

But before the shutter clicked, Emma's voice rang out, cutting through the air with urgency. "Wait! Ada should join us."

Mr. Lesesne raised an eyebrow, his brow furrowing in confusion. "But this is your wedding photograph. A child shouldn't be in it."

Emma shook her head vehemently, her determination shining through. "Yes, she should. I married into a family—Michael and Ada."

She turned to Ada, who stood nearby, nibbling on a chocolate croissant. The girl's eyes widened in surprise at the unexpected invitation, uncertainty flickering across her features. "I don't want to."

Michael motioned for her to join them, his gaze gentle yet persuasive. "Ada, sweetheart, come join us. You're part of this family."

Ada remained rooted to the spot, her resolve unyielding. He frowned as his daughter refused, and he grappled with conflicting emotions of failure, disappointment, and vexation.

In the end, Mr. Lesesne got his way, and Ada stayed out of the photograph. With a resigned sigh, he and Emma posed beside the magnificent wedding cake, their slight smiles masking the disappointment that lingered beneath the surface.

As the camera flashed, freezing the moment in time, Michael couldn't help but feel a pang of regret. Like Emma, he had hoped to capture their new family bond in the photograph, a symbol of their unity and love. But he reckoned that sometimes even the best-laid plans are thwarted by stubbornness and fear.

Their wedding photograph would forever remind him that something vital was missing—a piece of their family puzzle. But he held onto hope, for with time and patience, hopefully one day, their bonds would grow stronger, creating new memories that would endure for a lifetime.

Amid clinking glasses and heartfelt toasts, the wedding breakfast continued in a spirit of camaraderie and celebration.

But would Ada be the thread that breaks or binds? Only time would tell.

Chapter 4

The next afternoon, Emma stood outside the lighthouse cottage that would become her home. The billowing clouds overhead cast shadows across the landscape, painting the scene in shades of gray. The cool breeze tousled her hair, carrying with it the scent of the river and adventure.

A surge of excitement came with it at the thought of starting a new chapter of her life on this quaint island. Emma couldn't wait to move in. But beneath her excitement lurked a thread of apprehension, a nagging doubt about whether she was truly ready for this new beginning, especially after Ada's caustic reactions to her. Moving to a new place meant leaving behind the familiar comforts and companions of her old life, and the uncertainty of what lay ahead loomed large.

Suddenly, Ada ran past her, huffing and stomping up the porch steps and into the house, mumbling loud enough for Emma to hear, "This will be the worst summer ever."

Michael, who had been carrying Emma's steamer trunk, set it down and hurried after her. "What's wrong, darling? Are you all right?" Apparently, he hadn't heard his darling's remark.

Clutching her overnight case, Emma moaned as

Michael disappeared into the cottage, leaving her standing alone. She had expected him to carry her over the threshold, a romantic gesture she had daydreamed about. But instead, he had rushed off to tend to his daughter's needs first. Was this how it would be from here on out?

She steeled herself, climbed onto the porch, and stepped inside the cottage, the old wooden floor creaking beneath her feet. She'd been there just once, but she hadn't properly taken it in as she did now. The interior was cozy but sparse, with simple furnishings and a few framed pictures on the walls. Somehow, she'd make it a home.

She hovered awkwardly in the entryway, unsure of where to go. After a moment, Michael emerged from one of the rooms, a warm smile on his face. "Ah, there you are, darling. Come, let me show you to our bedroom."

Emma followed behind him, feeling like an unwelcome guest in her new home. The dimly lit hallway echoed with the soft click-clack of her heels as she made her way up the staircase. The bedroom was modest but tidy, with a large bed dominating the space. She tried to imagine herself living here, sharing this intimate space with Michael. But it all still felt so foreign.

Taking a deep breath, Emma pushed aside her doubts and focused on the present moment. She had chosen this path for a reason, and she was determined to see it through.

He planted a kiss on her cheek. "Be right back, love. I need to get your trunk before it rains."

She nodded. Her weathered trunk held all her worldly possessions.

As she surveyed the room, footsteps approached from behind. Ada joined her, a wrinkled nose making her disapproval evident.

"Is that all you have, a single trunk and that bag? I brought back more than that from school." Ada's tone was laced with a hint of superiority.

Emma forced a tight smile, her nerves prickling under the girl's scrutiny. "I don't need much. I have all I need." Her voice sounded small and defensive, though she tried to keep it light.

She shifted her overnight case to a more comfortable position, her fingers gently tracing the worn edges of the handle. The case held her most precious possession—a delicate porcelain cherub. Its tiny wings and innocent expression brought a sense of comfort, a tangible connection to the warmth of her grandmother's presence.

She could still hear the laughter that echoed through her grandmother's kitchen and the gentle lullabies that her grandmother used to sing. Still smell the comforting scent of freshly baked cookies. The cherub figurine had been a constant presence in her grandmother's living room, a witness to decades of shared stories and joys.

Ada's gaze lingered on her bag before she

spoke again. "Seems like you don't have much. Are you just one of those poor old maids trying to take advantage of my father?" Her tone was tinged with skepticism.

Emma's heart sank, but she understood the girl's apprehension. "No, Ada. I'm not trying to take advantage of anyone. I love your father, and I want to be a part of your lives. These trunks may not hold many material possessions, but they carry everything that's important to me."

Ada studied her for a moment longer before shrugging slowly.

Emma offered her a small smile. "I hope we can get to know each other better and become a real family."

Ada's expression softened slightly, and she shrugged again. "Maybe." She turned and went into a nearby room, which Emma gathered was the child's bedroom.

Nerves prickled down her neck and along her spine. How difficult would this be?

She glanced at the bed. She hadn't shared a room with someone since she was a girl. Growing up, she bunked in with her three sisters.

But never with a man.

Her pulse quickened at the memory of her wedding night at the Columbian Hotel. Michael had been such a patient and loving husband. The perfect beginning to their life together.

Michael returned and set down her trunk. He

smiled and raised an eyebrow. "What's in the case?"

Emma chuckled. "Just some essentials. Oh, and this." She opened the case to reveal the cherub figurine.

His eyes softened as he took in the delicate piece. "That's beautiful. Where did you get it?"

"It was my grandmother's. She gave it to me before she passed away." Emotions stirred at the memory, her gaze lingering on the figurine. "It's the only thing I have left of her."

He nodded as if understanding the significance. "I'm honored that you brought it here to our room. It can guard our cherished memories and be a symbol of the love that transcends generations."

The breeze blew through the open window, refreshing them as they stood together in the center of the cozy room. She wrapped her arms around his waist, hugging him tightly. "You're such a treasure, Michael. Thank you for opening your heart and home to me so generously." Her heart overflowed with gratitude.

He smiled down at her and gently kissed the top of her head, and she savored his closeness. "It's *our* home, my love. It's *our* room. Not mine. And my heart is yours as well."

He playfully tweaked her nose, and she couldn't help but giggle. Their sweet interaction was interrupted by a more passionate kiss that left her heart soaring with joy.

"Marriage is divine," she whispered, reveling in the warmth of the moment.

"Argh! It's so wrong!" The frustrated statement echoed down the hallway as Ada stomped away. She must've been watching them!

Ada's bedroom door slammed shut with a force that sent a shiver through the house, causing the cherub figurine to shimmy on the nearby table.

Emma and Michael exchanged bemused glances before sharing a knowing smile. Family life, it seemed, had its unexpected twists and turns.

"This might not be quite so easy . . ." Michael's eyes sparked with a mix of concern and amusement.

She laughed softly, resting her head against his chest. "Well, it'll be an adventure, that's for sure."

As they enjoyed another moment wrapped in each other's embrace, the echoes of Ada's protestations lingered in the air, a reminder that the journey of love and family was bound to be filled with both divine moments and unforeseen challenges.

Moments later, Ada reemerged from her room, her features contorted with barely contained fury. Her gaze bore into Emma, sharp and accusatory. "Papa, you can't let her stay in there." Her demand echoed off the walls of the hallway.

Michael turned to face his daughter. "Ada,

Emma is my wife now. She has every right to share this room with me."

The child's eyes flashed with defiance. "But this is your room, Papa! It's just not right for her to be in there with you."

Emma stepped forward, her voice gentle but firm. "I understand that this is a big adjustment for you. But your father and I are married now, and we need to share a room."

Ada's lips trembled as she fought back tears. "But Papa . . ."

For goodness' sake! How could Emma ease this child's angst? She placed a comforting hand on her shoulder, but Ada shook it off, so she moved back, giving the girl space. "How about this? I'll take the third bedroom for now, just until you're more comfortable with the idea of me being here."

Ada blinked three times, her expression softening. "Really? You'd do that?"

She nodded, offering the girl a reassuring smile. "Just for now."

Michael placed a hand on Ada's other shoulder. "This is only for a little while, and soon Emma will move into our room. Permanently. It's very kind of her to make this sacrifice, Ada. I hope you appreciate it."

With a nod, Ada wiped away her tears and stepped aside to let Emma and her father settle Emma into the third bedroom.

But with Michael working all night, and Ada in

the house so full of anger and animosity, when would Emma have any time alone with her new husband?

The next day, Michael ran into Stella at the Thousand Island Park mercantile as the midday sun shone brightly through the windows. "Good day to you, Mrs. Everson. How are you and your sister?"

"Fine. Just fine. How's married life?" Stella greeted him with a warm smile as she held a handful of yarn to purchase, but her expression quickly shifted to one of concern.

He grinned, switching a package of shoelaces to his other hand. "Just dandy. Emma is more than I could ever ask for."

Stella clicked her tongue and raised an eyebrow. "She most certainly is, but there's something I need to tell you."

At the woman's cautionary tone, his stomach clenched. "Is everything all right? Is Mary okay?"

Stella motioned for them to scoot to a quiet corner, away from several shoppers' listening ears. "It's about Ada. She said something to Mary when she stayed with us that . . . well, I think you may need to know."

With a sinking feeling, he nodded. "Go on."

Stella cleared her throat. "She told Mary she doesn't like Emma. In fact, she hates her because she's stealing you away from her."

He sighed. He had hoped for better from his daughter. After all, Ada was eleven and had been away at school for these four years now. Certainly, this change shouldn't be so difficult. And to share such opinions with others?

Stella pursed her lips before speaking again. "It's normal for a young girl to have mixed feelings about a new stepmother. But it's not okay for her to say hurtful things, especially to others. And Emma, being a dear friend to us, doesn't deserve to be disrespected like that."

Guilt and regret reared their ugly heads. He knew he gave Ada far too much room to speak her mind. He also knew blending their family wouldn't be easy. But he had to do whatever it took to ensure Ada's happiness and well-being, even if it meant navigating through challenges like this one.

But what about his wife? She needed his protection too.

His mind raced, grappling with the vitriol of Ada's words. He appreciated Stella's interest and honesty, yet he couldn't shake the incessant pang of guilt gnawing at him. Emma had entered their lives with nothing but kindness and warmth, and it was unfair for Ada to harbor such resentment toward her.

Taking a deep breath, he met Stella's gaze with a sense of resolve. "Thank you for telling me, Stella. I'll talk to Ada and help her understand that Emma isn't a threat."

Stella nodded, her expression softening. "I'm sure she just needs time, Michael. Adjusting to change can be hard, especially for someone her age. But don't let her manipulate you. Females are good at that, you know, and Ada seems to have an acute talent for it."

He squeezed Stella's hand briefly before turning to pay for his shoelaces and leave, already formulating a plan of action. He needed to have a heart-to-heart with Ada, to reassure her that she would always hold a special place in his life, no matter what changes occurred, but that it was unacceptable to air her grievances publicly or treat Emma with disrespect.

As he stepped back out into the midday sun, a renewed determination to navigate the complexities of blending their family with patience and understanding bolstered him. Above all, he vowed to protect the happiness of both his daughter and his precious wife, who deserved nothing less than his unwavering support and love.

When he returned home, the afternoon breeze filtered through the curtains of the living room, cooling the cozy space quite nicely as he joined Emma and Ada. His daughter sat curled up on the couch, her black cat purring contentedly in her lap. Michael directed a firm look at her. "Ada, I said that if you brought Midnight from Grandma's, you'd need to keep the cat in the workshop, sweetheart."

Ada looked up, her eyes wide with innocence. "Midnight is lonely stuck in the shop alone all day, and besides, he wanted to meet Emma. Don't we all need to be his family?"

Emma hesitated, glancing warily at the cat before reluctantly placing the book she'd been reading beside her on the table along with her spectacles. "I'm glad you have such a wonderful companion in Midnight, but I really don't think it's a good idea for me to be near him. I'm terribly allergic to cats. I think it's best if I keep my distance."

Michael leaned forward, prepared to support Emma. "Ada . . ."

But his daughter scooped up Midnight. She crossed the room and placed the cat on Emma's lap. "There, now you can see for yourself how friendly he is."

Emma's face paled as she stared at the cat on her lap. Almost instantly, her eyes began to water, and her nose started to twitch. She tried to suppress a sneeze, but it erupted from her anyway, loud and uncontrollable.

"See, Emma? He likes you!" Ada exclaimed.

Emma struggled to speak through her now-congested nose. "Ada, please, I really can't—*achoo!*—be around cats."

Ada shook her head. "But I've never known anyone to be allergic to Midnight. He's a nice cat."

He had to intervene. "Ada, take Midnight outside or to your room. At once!"

Ada blinked at his stern command, but she hurried to retrieve Midnight from Emma's lap. As Ada retreated with the cat, Emma rubbed at her watering eyes, trying to regain her composure. She glanced up at him, her gaze revealing both gratitude and frustration.

He sighed, torn between his daughter and his wife. He went over and crouched beside Emma, offering her a reassuring smile. "I'm sorry, my dear. We'll find a solution that will bring peace—hopefully, sooner rather than later."

She nodded. "I appreciate your support, but I can't shake the feeling of regret for disrupting Ada's life—with my allergy and with my presence. I'm sorry. I don't want to cause any problems."

He placed a gentle hand on her forearm, making his gaze soft. "You're not causing problems, love. We're a family, and we'll figure this out together."

They rose, and he drew her into his arms in the dimly lit living room, but the question of their predicament lingered. They would need to have a frank discussion with Ada about finding a compromise that respected both her love for Midnight and Emma's health needs. But for now, all he could do was enjoy Emma's comforting embrace. They'd face this new challenge as a united front.

When they gathered around the dinner table, the tension from earlier in the day remained palpable. Emma's eyes were still red-rimmed from her allergic reaction to Midnight, and Ada had been crying over the cat. Time to address the issue directly.

"Ada, Emma. We need to talk about Midnight."

Ada's gaze flickered with uncertainty. Emma kept her eyes lowered, her fingers tracing patterns on the tablecloth.

He directed his attention to his daughter. "I understand how much Midnight means to you, Ada. But we also need to consider Emma's health. Her allergy is serious, and we can't ignore that."

Ada's shoulders slumped slightly. "I'm sorry, Papa," she murmured, her voice tinged with regret. "I didn't mean to make Emma sick. I just wanted Midnight to feel at home."

Emma looked up, meeting Ada's apologetic gaze with a small smile. "It's okay, Ada. I know you care about Midnight, and I appreciate that. But maybe we can find a way for Midnight to have his space while also making sure I'm safe."

Michael nodded, relieved to see the beginnings of understanding dawn in Ada's eyes. "How about if Midnight stays in your bedroom? If you want to take him outside with you, carry him out so he doesn't get fur around the house. But he is not allowed to wander around inside."

Ada's eyes narrowed. "That's not fair! He shouldn't be imprisoned in my room or the shop just because you married *her*."

Again? His heart sank as Ada's words cut through the tentative harmony that had begun to settle over the dinner table. He knew this conversation wouldn't be easy, but he had hoped they could find a compromise that satisfied everyone. His girl could be as stubborn as Farmer Fred's bulldog.

"We have to consider everyone's needs here, Ada." He kept his voice calm, yet disappointment tinged it. "Emma's health is important, just like your love for Midnight."

Ada crossed her arms, her expression defiant. "But why does Emma's health have to come before my happiness? I need Midnight."

"No one is saying Midnight can't be part of the family." He tamped down his growing frustration. "We just need to live peacefully together, and that means making some adjustments."

Ada huffed, her frustration giving way to resignation. "Fine." She kept her gaze fixed on the table, but her tone was bitter. "I'll keep Midnight in my room."

He reached across the table, squeezing her hand reassuringly. "Thank you, darlin'. We'll make things work for everyone, I promise."

As they finished their meal in subdued silence, he couldn't shake the sense of unease between them. They still had a long way to go before they found true harmony, but he would do whatever it took to ensure the happiness and well-being of both his daughter and his wife, even if it meant navigating through other difficult conversations and compromises along the way.

But how many would it take to get there?

Chapter 5

A week later, the sound of raindrops tapping against the windowpane echoed through the parlor. Emma stood and stretched, restless energy coursing through her as the afternoon dragged on. The relentless downpour had forced her and Ada to stay indoors for the past two days, and the tension was thick as mud.

As usual, Michael slept through the morning and then headed to the shop to work on projects he had scheduled for the entire year. Her industrious husband's hands were always creating something, and she was proud of his work. But on days like these, she missed his buffering presence, his support, his companionship.

The lack of time alone with Michael began to take its toll on her. She felt isolated, and she longed for a sense of belonging on the tiny island. Doubts crept into her mind, whispering that perhaps she wasn't cut out for this life as a stepmother and lightkeeper's wife.

Though they had found time for a few solitary moments together, she longed for many more stolen moments of intimacy, yearning to express their love without interruption. After all, she was a new bride, right?

She sat back down on the sofa and reopened

her novel, her spectacles perched on the tip of her nose. Across the room, Ada fidgeted, her eyes fixed on the rain-soaked world outside. How could she engage a girl who didn't want to be engaged? Emma had read the same page twice pondering the dilemma.

"Emma, do you know why it's raining so much?" Ada's tone carried her usual hint of superiority.

She looked up from her book, furrowing her brow. "Well, sweetheart, rain happens when water vapor in the air condenses into droplets and falls to the ground. That's the basic concept, anyway."

Ada rolled her eyes, a smirk on her lips. Her dimples popped out as if to support her. "Basic for you, maybe. But can you explain the entire water cycle? I bet I know more about it than you."

Emma sighed, closing her book with a soft thud. "Okay, Ada. Enlighten me with your best science lesson."

With an air of confidence, the girl began her explanation, delving into the intricacies of evaporation, condensation, precipitation, and everything in between. Emma listened patiently, impressed by her knowledge, and occasionally nodding in acknowledgment. When Ada finished, the child stared at her triumphantly.

Emma leaned forward, forcing a small smile.

"You're a really smart girl. I did learn those things once upon a time. Now, let me share a story about the water cycle that might interest you."

She recounted a story that blended science with a touch of whimsy, weaving an intriguing tale about one little raindrop that made its way from the sea through the winds to the mountaintop and then into a tree.

Ada crossed her arms, still wearing a skeptical expression. But as the narrative unfolded, her eyes widened with curiosity. The girl even leaned in, and a half smile graced her lips.

"In time, the tree will release the water back into the air, completing the loop. Up, down, and all around—water is always in motion, shaping our landscapes, nurturing life, and connecting us all in this grand, cyclic dance." Encouraged by signs of softening, Emma caught the girl's eye. "Ada, come. I have an idea."

Ada sat up straight, her brow knitting. "What's your idea?"

She extended her hand toward the back room. "Shall we put your science to work in the kitchen? Baking and cooking are all about science, and I love to do both."

The girl's face lit up as she caught on to Emma's proposal. "That sounds like fun. Grandma's cook never let me in the kitchen, so I've never really thought about cooking that way."

Emma led the way to the kitchen, her steps light with excitement. "Oh, you'll be amazed at how much science is involved. From the chemical reactions that occur when ingredients mix to the precise measurements needed for baking, it's all science in action."

They gathered the ingredients for dinner and dessert from the pantry and icebox, and Emma explained each step to Ada along the way. "Take flour, for example." She held up the bag. "It contains proteins that, when mixed with liquid and kneaded, form gluten strands which give bread its structure and texture. Or in the case of Apple Betty, we use breadcrumbs."

Ada's brows raised as she absorbed the information eagerly. "So it's like a tiny science experiment every time you bake."

"Exactly." Emma's heart danced with joy at the connection. "And the best part is getting to taste the delicious results of your scientific endeavors."

Together, they set to work, measuring, mixing, and experimenting in the kitchen, their laughter filling the air as Ada discovered the wonders of science through the art of cooking. Perhaps the kitchen would be the key to the girl's heart. Oh, how Emma hoped so!

The rain continued its symphony outside, providing music to the unexpected bonding between the stepmother and stepdaughter. She, the bookworm, and Ada, the science enthusiast, were finding common ground.

As they worked, the aroma of simmering beef stew filled the kitchen, mingling with the sweet scent of apples from the oven. Emma hummed softly to herself as Ada stirred the stew. But why did the girl's expression remind her of a cat that had just caught a mouse?

Michael joined them as Emma ladled the stew into bowls and placed the golden-brown Betty on the table.

Ada's eyes lit up with excitement. "I made the Apple Betty, Papa, and helped with the stew too."

He chuckled "Did you, now? That's wonderful."

Ada eagerly dug into her stew, but as she took her first bite, her face contorted into a grimace. "Mama's stew was better."

Michael patted his lips with his napkin. "Ada, we don't compare one person's efforts to another."

Ada smirked, reaching for the saltshaker and adding a few more shakes to her stew before taking another bite.

Emma bit her bottom lip. Just when she thought she'd made progress . . .

Ada glanced at her and tilted her head. "You know, Emma, it's a shame you're Canadian and not American."

Emma paused, her fork hovering over her plate, surprised by the girl's comment. She took a bite of stew. Too much pepper. She didn't recall putting that much in it.

Michael shot his daughter a warning glance before turning his attention to Emma. He seemed as perplexed as she was.

Choosing her words carefully, Emma addressed the comment. "Well, Ada, I may be Canadian, but that doesn't make me any less capable or deserving of respect."

Ada shrugged dismissively, a smug expression on her face. "Sure, but being American is better. You know, with all the opportunities and stuff."

Michael huffed in exasperation. "Ada, that's enough. Emma is part of our family, and we treat each other with respect, regardless of nationality."

Ada lowered her gaze, chastened by her papa's reprimand.

Emma reached out, placing a reassuring hand on her husband's arm, silently thanking him for his support.

He winked, squeezing her hand in return. "We're a family, and we stand together, no matter what."

As they continued their meal, the atmosphere at the table lightened, the tension dissipating with each passing moment. Slowly, Ada made an effort to engage Emma in conversation, asking about her life in Canada and showing interest in her experiences.

But then, Ada's narrow-eyed glare revealed her condescension even before she spoke. "You know, Emma, I was just thinking about how different we are. You're more of a country girl, and I'm a city girl. We probably don't have much in common."

Emma paused, again caught off guard by Ada's comment.

Michael cleared his throat. "Let's not focus on our differences, Ada. We have plenty in common."

Ada pursed her lips dismissively, her gaze fixed on Emma as she addressed her father. "I'm just saying she probably doesn't understand city life like I do. All those museums, theaters, and fancy restaurants in Rochester. I doubt she's even been to many."

Emma kept her demeanor calm but determined. "Ada, whether I'm from the country or the city doesn't define who I am as a person. And, for your information, I grew up in a city. While our experiences may be different, it doesn't mean we can't find common ground and learn from each other. Just as we did while cooking together."

Ada rolled her eyes. "Sure, whatever you say, Emma."

"Let's try to find things we all enjoy, regardless of where we come from." Though Michael attempted to intervene again, his tone was weak.

Tired. "Emma, I know you have plenty of stories to share about your experiences, and Ada, I'm sure you do too."

After a second helping of brown Betty, Michael excused himself to light the lamp.

While Ada sat at the table drawing, Emma took the dishes to the sink, then chanced a look at the girl. "Ada, I noticed something during dinner tonight. It seemed there was a bit too much pepper in the stew."

Ada avoided her gaze, fidgeting with her pencil guiltily. "I . . . I'm sorry, Emma."

At least she didn't try to deny it. "Very well." Emma gave her a tentative smile. "It's important to own up to our mistakes, learn from them, and not repeat them."

Ada nodded and offered a remorseful grimace. "Sorry."

She went over and pulled Ada into a gentle hug. "I know you are, and I forgive you. Now, why don't we clean up the kitchen together, and maybe we can try making the stew again another day . . . without any extra pepper?"

Ada said nothing but rose and followed her to the sink to help. As they worked side by side washing and drying the dishes, the tension between them dissipated, replaced by a sense of camaraderie.

But how long would it be before the girl threw another obstacle in their path?

• • •

Michael stayed vigilant as the storm raged, the wind howling and the rain beating against the windows of the lighthouse. Inside, the warmth of the small lamp room offered safety from the tempest outside.

He stood by the window gazing out at the tumultuous river, his thoughts lost in the waves crashing against the rocky shore below. Hopefully, no one would be foolhardy enough to be out sailing on a night like this.

Emma entered the tower, her steps quiet against the creaking ladder. She paused halfway through the hatch, smiling at him for a moment before speaking. "Michael, can we talk?"

He turned to help her up into the room, his heart warming at the sight of her. "I'd love some company on a stormy night like this. What's on your mind?"

Her shoulders slumped, and her beautiful face was marred with worry. "It's Ada. I just don't know how to handle her."

She plunked down on the narrow bench, and he sat beside her, making his expression sympathetic. "She's had her struggles, but what bothers you?"

She patted her hair, her voice tinged with frustration. "She's so disrespectful, Michael. Every time I try to talk to her, she rolls her eyes and throws these hurtful, impertinent remarks at me."

He rubbed his earlobe, his heart sinking at her words. She was right. He should be defending her, protecting her. But he was torn between his daughter's pain—the pain he had inflicted on her by taking this job and sending her away and then remarrying—and Emma's. What was a man to do?

Instinctively, he defended his little girl. "I'm sorry, Emma, but she is dealing with a lot for a girl her age."

Emma reached out, placing a gentle hand on his arm. "I'm worried that you're coddling her too much. She mustn't be allowed to be disrespectful."

He raised his chin and straightened his spine. "Coddling her? What do you mean?"

She sighed, her frustration evident. "I mean, you talk to her, but then you comfort her, even protect her from the consequences of her sharp tongue."

He frowned, his defenses rising. "Ada's been through a lot. I just want to make sure she feels safe and loved."

"I know you do, Michael. But shielding her from the consequences of poor behavior won't help her in the long run. She needs to learn to hold her tongue and be respectful."

He sighed, running a hand through his hair. Emma was right, of course. But . . .

She patted his hand. "Part of being a parent is allowing children to make mistakes and learn from them. And . . . forgiving yourself when you make mistakes too. Mr. Wiseman told me that before we wed."

The tense silence between them that followed mirrored the storm outside and the turmoil within. Finally, he spoke, his words tinged with uncertainty. "I suppose you're right. I'll try to teach her to be more respectful." But would he lose Ada's love in the process?

Relief washed over Emma's face. "Thank you. I . . . guess I struggle to believe I am truly worthy of your love, that I am enough for you."

Truly? He would never have guessed a woman who seemed so confident disguised insecurity. He took hold of her trembling hands. "You are more than enough. You are a remarkable woman, filled with kindness, strength, and beauty."

Tears welled up in her eyes as she absorbed his words. "But am I? It seems that Ada means so much more to you."

"She's my daughter, Emma. It's a totally different kind of love."

"I know." She took a deep breath and continued, her voice steadier now. "But I've carried this fear for so long—believed it when others told me I'm not lovable. I'm afraid I'll end up being abandoned or hurt all over again."

He tightened the embrace to provide both comfort and validation. "I hope to prove those fears wrong, Emma. I love you deeply and completely. You deserve all the love, happiness, and joy that life has to offer, and I aim to give that to you."

As they sat together in the quiet of the lighthouse tower, the storm continued to rage outside, but inside, a sense of understanding began to take root. His Emma was a tender soul in need of his love.

The next morning, as the sun rose lazily over the horizon, painting the sky with hues of pink and gold, he waited at the cottage door for Ada, a fishing rod in hand. The storm had ended, finally, and it was time to fish as he and Ada had planned to do.

Emma came to the door of the kitchen, a dish towel in her hand. "Ada seems excited for your fishing trip."

"I wish you could join us, my love."

She waved off his concerns. "It's fine. You two need some time together."

Ada bounded down the stairs, her excitement unmistakable as she caught sight of him. "Morning, Papa!"

"Morning, darlin'." He flashed a grin at her. "Ready to go fishing?"

She nodded eagerly, her enthusiasm bubbling over. "You bet! Let's go catch some big ones!"

Michael kissed Emma goodbye, but as Ada and he made their way down to the rocky shore, he couldn't help but feel a pang of sadness at leaving Emma alone. "Ada, should we see if

Emma wants to join us? It could be a fun family outing."

Her smile faltered slightly, a shadow crossing her features. "I think it should be just us today."

He frowned, hoping she would renege. "Are you sure? I thought she might enjoy spending some time on the water with us."

Ada shook her head, avoiding his gaze. "Awww . . . Papa. It's just . . . I wanted to spend some time alone with you. Just the two of us. Like old times."

His heart softened at her words, understanding dawning in his heart. "Okay, let's make it a father-daughter fishing trip to remember."

Her smile returned, brighter than ever, as they made their way to the river's edge, the sound of water lapping against the rocks filling the air with a sense of peace and contentment. They climbed into the boat, and he rowed to their favorite fishing spot.

As the sun rose higher, casting a warm glow over the river, he and his daughter sat in the skiff beside each other, their lines cast out into the shimmering waters. The gentle sound of the waves lapping against the boat filled the air, a soothing melody for their quiet conversation.

"Ada, I wanted to talk to you about when I suggested Emma join us on the fishing trip."

She turned to look at him, curiosity shining in her eyes. "What about it, Papa?"

He ran a hand through his hair as he searched for the right words. "I realized you might want some one-on-one time with me sometimes."

Her expression softened, understanding dawning. "I like having you all to myself."

His heart swelled with love for his daughter. "I'm glad to hear that, Ada. But remember, the three of us are a family now."

She placed her hand on his arm. "I know you love me, and that's all that matters."

"Emma matters too." He wrapped an arm around her shoulders and took a deep breath, gathering his thoughts before speaking again. "I've noticed that lately, you've been a bit . . . short with Emma. Disrespectful. You roll your eyes, and your attitude toward her hasn't been very kind."

She shifted uncomfortably, her gaze dropping to the line in the water. "I guess I've just been frustrated with all this newness."

He nodded. "It's new for Emma, too, and she's part of our family now. When you're disrespectful toward her, it hurts her feelings."

She sighed, guilt washing over her features. "I didn't mean to hurt her."

Michael planted a kiss on the top of her head. "I'm sure you didn't, sweetheart. But I want you to try and be more careful with your words and actions toward her. She deserves to be treated with kindness and respect."

She nodded as she met his gaze. "I'll try to do better, Papa."

"That's my girl." He ruffled her hair. "I know that with a little effort, you'll be able to show Emma just how much you appreciate her."

As they sat together in the quiet of the boat, the sun rising high in the sky, their father-daughter bond felt stronger than ever. And though there would be challenges along the way, he was learning to deal with them better, thanks to Emma.

His wise wife.

When they returned from fishing with a stringer of five large fish, he took them to Emma in the kitchen. She looked up from preparing lunch, a curious smile playing on her lips.

He dropped a quick kiss on her soft lips before Ada came in. "I'm sorry I didn't invite you to come with us."

"It's fine. Really. Did you have fun together?"

He nodded, relieved by her understanding. "Yes, we did. Ada enjoyed the alone time with me, and I hope it helped." He leaned closer and whispered, "We also had a little talk."

"I'm glad." She smiled warmly and planted a return kiss on his whiskery cheek. "It's important for you and Ada to keep that special bond."

He sighed, the weight of guilt lifting off his shoulders at Emma's acceptance. "Thank you, sweetheart. I appreciate your understanding."

She squeezed his arm gently, her eyes filled with love and gratitude. "Of course. I'm just happy that you had fun and caught these fish. I'll prepare them for dinner."

Ada skipped into the kitchen. "Can I help cook them? Please?"

Michael beamed. Perhaps they'd turned a corner and their talk was already bearing fruit.

Chapter 6

The next morning, harsh sunlight filtered through the kitchen window, illuminating the mismatched chairs gathered around the sturdy wooden table. Emma's eyes watered as Midnight flicked his tail and rubbed against her leg, purring loudly. She turned her head away from her work and sneezed.

"*Achoo!*"

That fool cat had snuck out of Ada's room again. Or had he? As Ada entered the kitchen, a mischievous gleam in her eyes told the truth.

Emma tried in vain to keep her voice calm. "Ada, please! I need you to keep Midnight in your room. I can't handle the allergies."

Ada tossed her a reassuring smile. "Of course, Emma. I'll take care of it." But her tone held sarcasm, and her eyes hinted that she was plotting. Again.

Emma would have to talk to Michael again and have him to put a stop to this. But he was busy preparing for the lighthouse inspector's visit, and she didn't want to bother him. What was she to do until then?

She loved Ada, of course, and they'd had a good time making dinner last night. What had happened? The girl seemed bent on making her life miserable, and the disrespect, although not as overt, still remained.

She wiped her eyes on her apron before returning to her task, slicing the cabbage with precision, the sharp knife making quick work of the dense vegetable. The scent of vinegar hung in the air, intermingling with the earthy aroma of the ham hocks simmering on the stove.

Ada wrinkled her nose at the pungent smell. "What's that smell?"

Emma glanced up, a touch of apprehension catching in her throat. "Sauerkraut and ham hocks. Your father said it was his favorite." She tried to sound confident despite her uncertainty that the dish would turn out okay.

"Normally, yes." Ada smirked, waving a hand in front of her nose, as she headed out the door. "My grandmother makes the most amazing German dishes. She's a fantastic cook."

Emma's heart sank at the snub, disappointment washing over her. She had wanted to make something German for her husband and his special guest, the lighthouse inspector, but she was used to making Irish dishes. She prayed it tasted better than it smelled.

Precisely at noon, the inspector's boat chugged toward the dock. She watched from the window, smoothing down her apron and checking the pot of sauerkraut and ham simmering on the stove. She had spent hours preparing the meal, hoping to impress her husband and the lieutenant with her culinary skills. Would her cooking and housekeeping measure up, or would she embarrass her husband—and herself?

As the boat docked, the man stepped onto the wooden pier, his uniform crisply pressed and his demeanor official. Worry niggled at her nerves, so she lifted a prayer for mercy.

When Michael entered the kitchen with the inspector, Emma greeted him with a respectful curtsy and a forced smile, her heart pounding. She'd never met an inspector before, but Michael had described him perfectly.

"Welcome, Lieutenant Worthington." Emma tried to sound cheerful despite her nervousness.

Lt. Worthington nodded a greeting, his gaze sweeping over the kitchen with an observant eye. "Hello, Mrs. Diepolder. Pleased to meet you."

Ada paused in setting the table and beamed at the lieutenant, her eyes wide with admiration. She curtsied, her enthusiasm in stark contrast to Emma's nervousness. "Good afternoon, sir."

"Hello, Ada." Lt. Worthington gave her a small nod.

Emma gestured toward the table, where steaming plates of sauerkraut and ham hocks awaited them. "Please, have a seat, gentlemen. Lunch is served."

Worthington did as she bid, eyeing the meal with a skeptical expression. Once Michael blessed it, Emma held her breath, waiting for the inspector's reaction as he took a tentative bite.

The silence that followed was deafening. Emma's heart sank as Worthington's expression turned unpleasant, though he tried to hide it with a half smile. As she feared, the sauerkraut was too sour, and the ham hocks were too salty.

Michael smiled kindly at her, but his taut features betrayed him. "Thank you, Emma, for making my favorite meal. It's a difficult dish to master, I'm sure."

"Yes, thank you. I've not had German food before," Worthington remarked diplomatically, though there was a distinct lack of enthusiasm in his tone.

Emma's cheeks heated and her stomach tumbled while Ada watched the exchange.

The girl squared her shoulders and smirked. "You know, Lieutenant, my grandmother makes the most amazing German dishes. Her sauerkraut is always so flavorful, and her ham hocks are not so salty and practically melt in your mouth."

Tears threatened the back of Emma's eyes at the comparison, but she blinked them back.

Worthington nodded politely, though his expression remained sedate. "I like trying new dishes, and I'm sure your grandmother's cooking is quite delicious, Ada."

Michael pursed his lips at Ada before smiling at Emma. Then he turned to the inspector. "Emma is a wonderful cook, too, Lieutenant, but this dish isn't easy to make. Do you know the New Year's Eve tradition around it?"

The lieutenant shook his head, his brows furrowing as he took a small bite. "I don't, Michael. Please, enlighten me."

With a reminiscent glint in his eye, Michael said, "On New Year's Eve, when midnight strikes, the whole family gathers around the table. Laughter fills the room, excitement brimming, as we prepare for our cherished New Year's Eve tradition."

Ada's face lit up, and she put her hand in the air. "Let me tell the rest, please? Papa gives each of us a fork and a silver dollar. At the stroke of midnight, we hold the silver dollar in our left hand to symbolize hope for prosperity while we eat a forkful of sauerkraut to help bring us good health."

Lt. Worthington grinned. "That's quite a tradition."

Emma smiled, regaining a touch of peace in the process. "I've never heard of that tradition either. Guess I'd better master the dish before the New Year."

"You won't." Ada shrugged, superiority tainting her words. "But don't feel bad. You're not German."

After giving Ada a scolding head shake, Michael broke the tension by speaking again. "I was born in Germany, you know, and we had many traditions we held dear. One of my favorites was the celebration of Oktoberfest where the whole village would come together to feast, dance, and raise a toast to good health and happiness. Many of the German immigrants brought their traditions with them to this country."

Ada's eyes shone as Michael described the vibrant festivities of his childhood. "Will you take me there one day, Papa?"

Michael nodded. "I'd love to take both of my girls."

Ada rolled her eyes and pouted.

Emma smiled at Michael's acknowledgement of her. "I'm Irish, and we have different customs and celebrations. From St. Patrick's Day events to traditional Irish music sessions in the local pub, there's always something to look forward to. And of course, there's nothing quite like a proper Irish stew or a slice of soda bread to warm the soul on a cold winter's day."

Lt. Worthington sat up straighter. "Aye, I know a thing or two about Irish traditions myself. My parents grew up in County Cork. They told me about lively gatherings and folk festivals. Buffalo, where I now live, has many Irish immigrants who have brought those traditions with them."

"German traditions sound much more fun than Irish ones." With a smug look, Ada pushed her plate aside, having succeeded in putting a damper on the sense of fellowship that had finally begun to settle over the dinner. "May I please be excused, Papa? I can't eat this."

Michael shrugged, snapping an apologetic glance at Emma. "Go ahead, sweetheart."

They finished their meal in awkward silence, and Emma couldn't shake the feeling of failure that hung over her like a dark cloud. Despite her best efforts, she had fallen short of her own expectations. Would she ever be able to live up to the standards of being a lighthouse keeper's wife—or a proper stepmother?

Later that evening, when Michael had gone up in the tower to work, Emma started sneezing uncontrollably as she entered her room. The cat lay curled up on her bed, looking quite pleased with himself. Ire rose as she realized what Ada had done.

"Ada!" Emma hollered as she marched out of her room to find the girl.

Ada poked her head out of her bedroom door as Emma approached. "What's wrong, Emma?" With wide, blinking eyes, she feigned ignorance.

"You know exactly what's wrong, young lady. I asked you to keep Midnight in your room because of my allergies, and now he's in mine!"

Ada's grin widened as she struggled to contain her laughter. "Well, technically, I did keep him in my room. I just didn't keep him there the whole time. Besides, this is his house too."

Emma's frustration turned into disbelief at Ada's cunning interpretation of her request. She shook her head in exasperation as she fixed Ada with a withering glare. "Your father will most certainly hear about this flagrant act of disobedience, young lady." Her voice was sharp, dripping with disapproval. "Mischief may be tolerated to a degree, but this kind of blatant disregard for the rules is unacceptable."

Ada had the good sense to look chastened, though a glimmer of defiance still flickered in her eyes. "I'm sorry. I was just—"

"Sorry?" Emma interrupted, her tone allowing no argument. "Sorry does not undo the disrespect you have shown." She gestured sharply toward the door. "Now remove that wretched creature at once, and pray your father is in a forgiving mood when I inform him of your transgressions."

Ada swallowed hard, the color draining from her face. She hurried to scoop up the cat, who let out an indignant yowl at being disturbed. As she headed for the stairs, she cast a nervous glance over her shoulder.

Emma blew out a ragged breath. What was she to do with that girl?

Michael escorted Lieutenant Worthington across the grounds of Rock Island Lighthouse, the inspector's keen eyes taking in every detail as he studied the smokehouse and carpenter's shop.

Worthington paused beside the smokehouse, running a hand along the freshly painted wall. "Impressive work, Michael. Your smokehouse is in excellent condition."

He nodded gratefully, his chest swelling with pride at the praise. "Thank you, Lieutenant. It's served us well over the years."

Moving on to the carpenter's shop, Worthington examined the tools and equipment with a critical eye. "And your carpenter's shop seems to be well-stocked and organized. You've done a fine job maintaining it."

"Yes, sir. We do our best to keep everything in working order. You never know when you might need to make repairs around here."

As they continued their inspection, Worthington's gaze fell upon the well, and he motioned toward it. "How's the well working? Any issues with water supply?"

Michael shook his head and gave the pump a firm pat. "No, sir. The well has been working perfectly fine. We installed the new pump last year, and it's been running smoothly ever since."

Worthington smiled, his expression turning thoughtful. "And I see you've dug a root cellar as well. That's a wise investment, especially for storing perishable goods."

Michael's pulse ticked up a notch at Worthington's commendation. "Yes, sir. The board's improvements have been a blessing to us in the past few years. The fertile soil brought in to cover the bare rock has sure helped. And though it took a few years to coax the grass to grow, it's thriving now."

Worthington scanned the lush green grass that now covered the once-barren rock. "Well done, Michael. It seems you've made some significant improvements to the grounds here at Rock Island Lighthouse. Keep up the good work."

The inspector glanced up at the lighthouse as he prepared to inspect the light tower. He scratched his chin. "I don't understand why this tower is still set so far back on the island. After the *A.E. Vickery* shipwreck in '89, we can't afford to take any chances with the safety of our navigational aids."

Michael nodded solemnly, his mind racing with hope it would change. "I agree, Lieutenant. Moving the lighthouse out to the shore or raising it would greatly increase its visibility and reduce the risk of future accidents, as I've mentioned every year in my report to the board."

Worthington sighed, running a hand through his hair. "Take heart, Michael. There's a plan to help, at least in the short term. In the fall, the platform will be raised by five feet. Workers will set it atop a solid octagonal wall of granite laid in Portland cement with sufficient mortar beneath. That should significantly increase the visibility from the water. But we'll continue to push for approval to move the lighthouse out to the shore permanently. As you're well aware, such decisions require approval from higher authorities, and the bureaucratic process can be slow-moving at best."

Michael shook his hand. "Thank you, Lieutenant. Any improvement will help to keep folks safe."

As they walked back to the cottage, Lieutenant Worthington stopped and stared at the house. He looked at the ground. "Michael, I do have an immediate concern. May I be frank?"

"Of course, Lieutenant."

He glanced at the cottage, leaning closer to Michael and lowering his voice. "I'm pleased to see you and your wife are so happy, but I must admit, I'm a bit worried."

Michael swallowed, waiting for Worthington to continue. What could be troubling him? Did he notice the tension between Emma and Ada?

"It's about Emma. Since she's Canadian, I fear the lighthouse board may not take kindly to having a foreigner in a government position. They can be sticklers on such things."

Michael's chest tightened. "She's lived in TI Park for eight years, which is American, you know. You needn't worry about Emma. She's as much a part of this community as anyone else, and I'm sure she'll be willing to do whatever it takes to prove herself."

Worthington's gaze softened with empathy. "I'm not personally worried, and I appreciate your loyalty to your wife, Michael. But the reality is, the lighthouse board may not see it the same way. On paper, she's Canadian living in an American lighthouse. You are seen as one team."

Michael took a deep breath before revealing his own immigrant past. "My family immigrated to the United States when I was just six years old. I became a naturalized citizen when I turned twenty-four, and I've never looked back. If I can do it, so can Emma."

Worthington's respect shone in his gaze. "Thank you for sharing that with me."

"Ada's mother, Mary, passed away in February of 1886. I took on the position of lightkeeper here in September of that year, and Ada has to live with her grandparents during the school year and only comes home on weekends and holidays when she can. It hasn't been easy for either of us, but I'm sure Emma's presence will prove a blessing for all of us, including the work she does here."

Worthington nodded, a newfound understanding dawning in his eyes. "It sounds as though you've been through a lot, Michael. I'll notate these comments and vouch for you. I have no doubt that you and Emma will find a way to overcome any obstacles, including bureaucracy."

After Lieutenant Worthington left, Michael

joined Emma on the porch settee, worry about his position pressing on him. Emma sat next to him and held her breath as she watched him wrestle with his thoughts.

"Michael, what's wrong?" She touched his arm.

He sighed heavily. "It's Worthington. He's worried about us."

Her eyes widened and brows furrowed. "Worried about us?"

He hesitated for a moment before speaking. "About you, actually." Despite his efforts to remain calm, anxiety tinged his voice. "About you being Canadian."

She gasped. "Oh, Michael, I didn't realize that would be a problem. I'd never want to put your job at risk."

He shook his head, searching her eyes. "I didn't know, either, and it's not your fault, my love. But the truth is, the lighthouse board may not take kindly to having a foreigner in a government position. And if they decide to replace me because of it . . ."

His voice trailed off as he was unable to finish the thought. The idea of losing his position as lightkeeper, the only stability he and Ada had known since Mary's passing, filled him with dread.

Emma took his hand and gave it a reassuring squeeze. "We'll find a way to make it work, darling. We're a team."

He forced a weak smile, grateful for her unwavering support. "I know, Emma. But it's not just about us. It's about Ada too. I can't bear the thought of uprooting her again."

She nodded. "We'll fight for our home, Michael. Together."

As they sat in the quiet of the waning day, uncertainty still clung to him. He held Emma's hand, drawing strength from their love and her determination to weather whatever storms lay ahead.

As the sun began to sink into the western sky, he lit the white signal lantern hanging from the corner of the porch, its soft glow casting a warm light against the soon-to-come darkness. Building clouds warned of a summer storm.

"You know, Emma, this lantern holds a special significance for me."

She turned to look at him, curiosity shining in her eyes. "What do you mean?"

He gestured toward the light with a fond smile. "This lantern is used during the summer hotel season, from sunset to sunrise. It's hung in the direction of the Thousand Island Park dock because during those months, the light from the tower is often obscured by the roof of the keeper's dwelling when viewed from Thousand Island Park. When we were courting, I lit it in hopes of you being here, with me, one day."

Her eyes sparkled, the setting sun lighting her

face. "I saw it, Michael, and hoped the same. But can this small lantern really help guide boats safely to shore when the lighthouse's light is not visible?"

"As small as it is, yes. It's an extra way to ensure the safety of those navigating the waters around us."

Ada joined them, wrapping an arm around her father. "What are you talking about, Papa?"

He enfolded her with a hug and kissed her forehead. "We're talking about the importance of this lantern, sweetheart."

Ada looked up at the lantern and smiled. "I heard, and that's a really smart idea, Papa. But I thought it was for us."

"For all of us, darlin'. For the three of us and all those who sail the river."

For a moment, the three of them sat together on the veranda. Bathed in the warmth of the lantern, they enjoyed a mutual moment of peace. Looking at the lantern, he smiled at the simple yet profound ways in which they could make a difference in the lives of others.

Before heading to the tower, Michael bid his wife and daughter goodnight. "I'd better get to my post. Looks like a storm might be coming. Sleep well, dear ones."

Though it was hard to leave them each evening, as long as they had each other, they'd be okay.

As Michael lit the lamp, the question about

Emma's nationality still niggled at him. Yet the inspector had promised to vouch for them. Surely, they could rely on him to make things right, just as he worked tirelessly for the safety of those on the river.

Michael was even more grateful for a supportive and loving wife. And while Ada had her moments of mischief and a sharp tongue, it seemed she and Emma were slowly bonding. Then why did his sense of foreboding refuse to budge?

Chapter 7

Far past midnight, frustration still gnawed at Emma as lightning lit her bedroom, warning of the impending storm her husband had mentioned. Compared to the growing tempest inside her, a summer storm would be refreshing. The possibility of her Canadian heritage putting Michael's career in jeopardy haunted her thoughts.

But more than that, Ada's continual defiance set her nerves on edge and tainted every day. For three weeks, Emma had been trying to navigate the ups and—mostly—downs of life with Ada. The mischief she could handle, but the latest incident with Midnight was a tipping point.

She had tried so hard to be the wife and stepmother that Michael and Ada deserved, pouring her heart and soul into this new life on the isolated island. Each morning, she would rise early, taking time to pray and seek God's guidance. She asked for the wisdom and patience to navigate the challenges of her roles, to find a way to connect with Ada and be the nurturing presence the young girl needed. And she longed to be the wife Michael needed too. Her faith had always been a source of strength, and she clung to it now more than ever, hoping it would see her through.

And yet, despite her best efforts, she still felt like an outsider. She longed for intimate interludes with Michael, free of Ada's interruptions and influence. Yes, they've stolen a few moments alone, and she enjoyed every kiss, but she wanted to feel like a newlywed.

Instead, she felt like a huge failure—as a wife and a mother.

She swiped at her still-itchy eyes and whispered into the darkness. "Something has to be done, or I'll not sleep a wink!"

Donning her robe and smoothing her rumpled hair, she stepped into her house shoes and headed toward the lighthouse. For a moment, she stopped to listen at Ada's bedroom door. Silence. That was good. At least when the child slept, she'd not be getting into mischief.

Emma hurried down the stairs and out the back door, dodging a few raindrops during the twenty paces from the cottage to the lighthouse. She quietly climbed the lamp room ladder and found Michael engrossed in the tried-and-true epic sea story, *Moby Dick*. He didn't even notice she'd come.

"Good evening, Michael." Her tone was flatter than she'd meant it to be, ire leaking into her words.

Michael jolted from his book, blinked several times, and gasped, as if he'd seen a ghost. Then a grin lit his handsome face just as another lightning flash illuminated the lamp room. He stood and motioned for her to sit on the narrow bench beside him. "What in heaven's name are you doing up at this hour, my lovely wife?"

She took a seat next to him and bit her bottom lip, trying to keep the frustration out of her tone. "We need to talk about Ada. Again."

A groan slipped out of his lips, his grin turning to a frown. "What now?"

A loud thunderclap made her jump, causing her heart to beat wildly and her emotions to flutter with it. Why did she have to keep revisiting the same problem over and over? Seemed that was all they talked about. She wanted to talk about God and the deep things of marriage and intimacy, of hopes and dreams and plans for the future, of what she was reading.

But Ada always took precedence. Perhaps that was the way it should be, but she had to admit that it was disappointing.

"When I went upstairs tonight, Midnight was sleeping on my bed. I talked to Ada about it, and I've told her a dozen times to keep the cat in her room, but she outright disobeys. It's disrespectful, Michael, and the cat makes me ill."

He sighed, narrowed eyes and a slight shake of his head hinting exasperation. "She's just a child with an itch to be mischievous. She's always enjoyed pulling harmless pranks, darling. She probably thought it was funny."

"Funny? It's not a joke, Michael. My eyes itch and lungs fill up within moments. Hours later, they still itch. That cat sheds hair all over the place, and now it's all over my bedding. Ada needs to learn some respect and obedience."

Michael leaned back against the wall. "I'm sorry, sweetheart. How about you sleep in my bed? *Our* bed, Emma."

Emma's heart beat wildly. Perhaps things would finally change. "Seriously? That'd be wonderful, Michael. But we still have to solve the problem with Ada. She's more than impish. She's contrary and headstrong—all with an innocent smile. It's maddening."

"She's testing her boundaries with you, Emma. I'm sure every child does this, especially with a stepparent. But you've never been a parent, so I wouldn't expect you to know about that."

His dismissal pinched her heart. Why couldn't he understand? Why wouldn't he support her?

Tears pricked the back of her eyes, but she blinked them back. "I've worked with plenty of children in the library and elsewhere. This goes far beyond testing boundaries, Michael. She's blatantly disobeying and disrespecting me." Her voice sounded whiny, even to her own ears.

He took her hand and patted it gently with the other. "Sweetheart. Please understand. It's been less than a month since the wedding, and she's still adjusting to this big change. So are you.

Give her some time. Please. She hasn't had to share me for over four years."

Another lightning strike flashed, and a thunderclap followed close behind. She wasn't going to convince him of anything tonight. Her stomach flipped in resignation. "I'd better get back to the cottage before the clouds burst and soak me clear through."

He tilted her chin toward him and kissed her soundly. "Be patient, my love. We'll get through this. She'll adjust. But for now, please sleep in my bed—our bed—tonight."

"When will it truly be *our* bed? It's been over three weeks."

He kissed her again, this time deeper, just as he did on their wedding night. She missed that. Wanted that. Hungered for that. She melted into his arms, kissing him back.

Michael gave a rough sigh. "It has been three *long* weeks, I agree. That changes tonight, Emma."

She sat up straight and stared into his piercing brown eyes. "Really? Really and truly, Michael?"

"Really. And tomorrow, I think we should all get away for the day, and we'll tell her then. I'd like to take you both to Sister Island to meet the Dodges. It should be a refreshing outing for all of us."

Emma threw her arms around his neck. "Oh, thank you, dearest. That'll be wonderful. Perhaps

Ada will finally understand that we are truly married. That we can be a family."

His gaze flickered with doubt, and she wanted to say more. But then the rain began a steady, heavy march on the lamp room glass, calling their attention to the impending torrent. "You'd better get inside while you can, Emma."

She giggled. "I'd rather stay here, in your arms."

He embraced her tightly and whispered into her hair. "Oh, how I wish you could. But I have work to do, and we can't leave Ada alone in a storm. I'm afraid that she tends to be quite frightened of them."

Emma smirked. "I didn't think she'd be afraid of anything. Ada is such a strong little lass."

"She acts strong and tough to cover her fears and insecurities, I think." A thunder boom rattled the panes of glass this time, and Michael gave her a gentle nudge. "Go, my love. We'll talk with her tomorrow."

He planted one more passionate kiss on her lips before sending her off. That would get her through the night.

Reluctantly, she hurried toward the ladder, but before she descended, he brushed her cheek with the back of his hand. "I love you, Mrs. Emma Diepolder. With all my heart."

She needed that. "I love you, too, Michael. Goodnight."

When she got to the bottom of the lighthouse,

the rain was already coming down in sheets. "Oh heavens!" She tucked her head, lifted her skirts, and ran to the cottage as fast as she could. She'd be drenched, for sure.

When she entered, muffled screaming filled the air. Ada!

What was happening? Was she hurt?

Emma flung off her shoes, ignored her wet clothes, and scurried up the steps to Ada's room. She found the girl under her covers screaming, "Help me! Stop! Stop the storm! Help me!"

"I'm here, Ada. It's okay." She pulled the girl from under the blankets and into her arms.

Ada wrapped her arms around Emma's middle and held on tight. "I hate storms. The thunder. The lightning. I cannot sleep alone. Papa and Grandma always let me sleep with them during thunderstorms, but they're not here. I can't be alone in a storm. I just can't."

Emma smoothed her rumpled hair and gave her a squeeze. "I don't care for storms either. Let's climb into your papa's bed and snuggle in together. How does that sound?"

Ada pulled back and stared at her as if she spoke a different language. "In Papa's bed?"

A pang of disappointment swept over Emma when she realized Ada would be in their bed when Michael came in the morning. But Emma stood and gently tugged the child to her feet. "It was your papa's idea."

A huge grin rose on the girl's face, and she ran to her father's bed, jumped on it, and slipped under the covers as Emma took off her wet robe, praying the child would welcome her comfort.

For several moments, Ada held the covers tightly around her neck as if to keep Emma out. But when another huge thunder boom shook the house, she flipped the covers back.

Before the child could change her mind, Emma joined Ada in the bed that should rightly be her own. She ran her hand on the crisp sheets she'd washed and ironed that day, but when thunder rumbled and lightning flashed yet again, Ada grasped Emma's hand and clung to her, shaking like a leaf.

Emma smoothed her hair. "There, there. I'm here. I will always be here for you. There's no need to fear."

Ada groaned. "You can't promise that. Lila's parents were killed in a storm, and she became an orphan." The girl whimpered, unconsciously admitting the reason for her fear.

Emma's stomach churned, empathy growing in her. She kept her tone soft, gentle. "I'm so sorry to hear that, Ada, but such a tragedy rarely happens. Who is Lila?"

Ada wiped the tears from her cheeks with the back of her hand. "She's my friend at school. She lost her parents when lightning struck their house and burned it down, and now she lives with her nasty old-maid aunt when she's not in boarding school with me."

"Goodness. Well, I'm glad she has you as a friend, but don't worry about the storm. Your papa won't let anything happen to us. Now, why don't we get some sleep, and before you know it, it'll be morning and the storm will have passed."

Ada's brows furrowed for a moment, but then she yawned, not bothering to cover her mouth. "I . . . I guess you're right. Thanks . . . for being here." With that, she rolled onto her side, turning her back to Emma.

Emma held in her surprise. "You're most welcome. I'll always be here for you, Ada. No matter what."

The child didn't respond, and within moments, Emma heard the rhythmic rise and fall of sleep-rendered breathing.

She'd be there for Ada, but would peace and acceptance ever truly join them on that journey?

Once the sun rose, Michael extinguished the light and entered a quiet cottage ready for breakfast and their excursion to Sister Island. Emma was always up at the crack of dawn, ready to greet him with coffee on the stove and a smile on her pretty face.

Instead, the stove sat cold. Were Emma and Ada all right?

Nerves prickled and blood surged in his veins. He climbed the stairs two steps at a time to find both Emma's and Ada's doors wide open and their beds empty.

Where were they?

His bedroom door was closed, as always. Perhaps one of them was in there? But where was the other?

He opened the door to find the quilt a lumpy mess. His girls couldn't both be there—together—could they? Unfathomable! Ada barely tolerated Emma these days. Even in a storm, his daughter wouldn't invite Emma's comforting embrace. Would she?

No one stirred, so he tiptoed nearer to the bed. Sure enough, Emma and Ada slept peacefully. He gazed at them for several moments, admiring the two beauties before him.

They could pass for mother and daughter, for sure. At least in their looks.

Their personalities, however, were another story. Emma, the quiet, peaceful one. Ada, the headstrong, feisty one. Would the three of them ever become a happy, loving family?

Emma's eyes fluttered open, and she licked her lips sleepily. A tiny smile lit her face when she saw him staring at her.

Oh, how he wished he could join her, hold her, be with her! Alone.

She silently slipped out from between the covers and donned her robe that awaited her on the nearby chair. Then she rose up on her tiptoes, kissed him on the cheek, and whispered, "Good morning, husband." Her breath tickled his ear, and her eyes danced.

Taking her hand, he gently tugged her out of the room and closed the door. "Let's let Ada sleep a few more minutes."

Emma nodded. "Sorry I overslept. I know you want to leave. I'll get ready quickly."

Michael touched her cheek. "It's okay. I'll start the fire. We'll set out for Sister soon."

Within minutes, he had the stove lit and coffeepot on it, just as he'd done for so many years before Emma came. She entered the kitchen, dressed in a soft yellow dress and her hair up in a pretty, loose chignon. He grinned. "You look lovely, wife. And you're especially beautiful when you first wake up, too—in *our* bed."

She giggled. "Stuff and nonsense, but thank you, Michael. When do you want to leave?"

He poured the coffee and bid her to sit. "Within the hour. I'll borrow Ed Green's wagon, and we'll rent a skiff in Chippewa Bay. It'll be fun."

Emma's eyes lit up like fireworks but dimmed just as quickly. "But you haven't slept, and it sounds like a long day. You must be tired."

"The thought of being with you is all the rest I need. I can nap later. Let's have a few minutes together before Ada wakes." He plunked down on a chair and rubbed his whiskers. "Guess I should shave."

"And I should prepare for the trip. But first, I want to tell you about last night." Emma did just that, sharing the amazing drama of Ada receiving comfort from her. Tears filled Emma's silvery eyes that sparkled even more with the wetness. His heart clenched at the hopefulness he sensed in her. Hope, he prayed, that wouldn't be thwarted by his little spitfire's changing moods, moods that had become more frequent and fervent than they had ever been.

They talked about how to tell Ada about their plan to move Emma into his room for good. Ada would likely fuss, but he had determined to remain firm. For all their sakes.

He took a sip of coffee and sighed. Though he could command his body to endure the grueling nights as lightkeeper, navigate the rough and stormy river to rescue someone in need, or dig a root cellar five feet into the rocky ground, when it came to his daughter, his resolve melted like a chunk of ice in the August summer sun.

No! He'd have to stay strong.

Ada entered the kitchen in a flurry of emotions. "Where's Midnight?" Her question was loud and shrill and fearful. "I . . . I forgot about him 'cuz of the storm."

Before Michael had the chance to speak up, Emma did. "Don't worry, Ada. We'll find him. He was probably scared, too, and he's hiding." Her tone held compassion and grace.

He smiled and his throat thickened. He and his daughter were blessed to have Emma in their lives.

"But you're allergic." Ada's voice held a softness he hadn't heard since she came home from school.

Emma waved a hand. "I don't have to touch him. Just help you find him. Let's go."

They did. Together. Without him.

He followed them up the stairs and into Ada's room, for he had to see this amiable interaction for himself. If it took a thunderstorm to change his daughter's attitude, then he was grateful for the stormy night.

Ada glanced around her room, a frown marring her sweet face. She bent down, peeked under the bed, and nodded. Her face lit up, then she put her index finger to her lips and smiled. She rose and shooed them from her room, whispering, "He's all right. Sleeping peacefully under my bed. Come on. I'm hungry."

Crisis averted, they headed back to the kitchen for a hearty bowl of oatmeal, which Emma whipped up in no time.

Michael took a sip of his lukewarm coffee while Ada gulped her milk. He cleared his throat. "How would you like to go for an outing, Ada? I'm sure you're ready to get off the island."

She licked her lips. "Would I? Yes, please. It gets lonely out here on the island. It is pretty and all, but at school, I have lots of girls to play with and talk with. Here, all I have is Midnight and my books."

He shrugged, ignoring her negativity. "Then we'll head out right after breakfast."

And they did.

On the trip to Sister Island Lighthouse, he almost told Ada about their plan to change Emma's room, but he decided to wait and discuss it on the way back. He didn't want his daughter airing their private affairs to the Dodges.

But he did share about his fellow keepers. "The Dodges have been keeping Sister Island Lighthouse for twenty-four years. William became the keeper last year after his father passed away from dropsy of the heart. His mother still lives on the island with him. Sister is very different than Rock Island Lighthouse, as you'll see. It's really three tiny islets joined together into one long string of islands right in the middle of a wide part of the St. Lawrence, halfway between Canada and America."

Emma grinned. "Really? Sounds enchanting."

Ada folded her arms and pouted. "And boring. There aren't any kids there?"

He hated disappointing her. "Sorry. No. But it'll be fun to discover a new place, don't you think? You'll have a good time, and I promise, I'll take you to play with Mary at Thousand Island Park soon, okay?"

Ada shrugged. "Okay."

He tossed her a wink before continuing. "One of the reasons I wanted to go there was because Lieutenant Worthington reminded me of the steamer-and-barge collision they experienced last month. I need to find out what William has learned."

Emma's eyes grew wide. "Goodness! Was everyone all right?"

He shook his head. "One man died, but the Dodges saved many. It sounded quite dramatic."

After renting a skiff in Chippewa Bay, he rowed to Sister. All the way, Ada moped and was unusually silent.

His failure as a father threatened to overshadow the anticipation of their visit to Sister. This summer was not how he hoped it would be. How could he make the child happy when he had duties to perform and a wife his daughter didn't like?

Chapter 8

As they approached Sister Island, Emma's stomach churned. Would Mrs. Dodge approve of a Canadian old maid serving with her husband in an American lighthouse? Before the inspector raised his concerns, she hadn't considered that her heritage might be a problem. Now, it hovered over her like a swarm of gnats. Added to that, her challenges with Ada, and the day could turn out badly.

"Isn't she a beauty?" Michael cut into her thoughts as he tipped his chin toward the lighthouse. The limestone, two-story keeper's house was magnificent, and the light tower popped out of the middle of the charming cottage like a steeple on a church. A wooden boathouse stood nearby, and a few trees were scattered about, but that was all. The long, narrow island's isolation made her shiver.

"Are you chilly, Emma?"

She grinned. "No. I was just thinking how remote this place is. It must get lonely."

"Especially if you're a kid. Who would ever want to live here?" Ada spoke for the first time since they entered the skiff.

Michael clicked his tongue. His daughter hadn't said a cheery thing all day. "The Dodges do. The new lightkeeper grew up on the island while his father kept the light. William loved it so much that he took the keeper's position after his father passed last year. So be nice, please, and be on your best behavior while we're with them."

Ada rolled her eyes but said nothing. Her sour attitude was a stark change from the warm embrace of last night. What if she revealed the tension between them to the Dodges? Would Michael support his wife or child?

As they drew nearer to the island, three people stood on the dock waiting for them. The man had to be the keeper, William Dodge. He was tall and handsome with a wide grin and dark, curly hair. The older woman had to be his mother, Mrs. Dodge. She was tall and thin, too, with wispy white hair.

"Who's the young woman, Michael?"

He shrugged. "I have no idea, but we'll soon find out."

As they stepped from the skiff, a stiff breeze yanked Emma's hat, so she clamped her hand onto it and held it there. Would the Dodges accept her or dismiss her as an outsider? She took a deep breath, steeling herself for the meeting.

William shook Michael's hand, glanced at Ada, and nodded to Emma. "Welcome, friends!" He placed his hand on the young woman's forearm. "Julia, I'd like you to meet the Rock Island lightkeeper, Michael Diepolder, his daughter, Ada, and his new bride, Mrs. Emma Diepolder. This is Julia, a dear friend who is visiting us for a while."

Emma curtsied. "Mr. Dodge. Mrs. Dodge. Thanks for having us."

Mrs. Dodge grinned. "Please call us Dee and William. May I call you Michael and Emma? Being fellow keepers, we're practically family!"

Michael shook her hand. "Of course."

Emma nodded. Her heart sped up as she wondered at the young woman. Those warm brown eyes and thick, luxurious hair with its reddish hues. Confident and beautiful. Petite and thin, just like . . .

She held her breath as memories skittered through her mind like lightning strikes. "You resemble someone I once knew and loved. Your vibrant ginger eyes, just like hers. Your smile the spitting image of her. I . . . I miss her." A shadow of sadness flickered in her heart, a ghost from the past reminding her of what she'd missed all these years. What she had lost.

Julia tilted her head curiously but shifted her attention to Ada. "Ada, is it? My, but you're a pretty little thing."

Ada clung tightly to her father's hand and scowled. Her gaze darted between the adults, and her nose wrinkled. "I'm not little or a thing. I'm eleven." She rolled her eyes and pointed to the cottage. "This lighthouse is so much different than ours, Papa. But it's far too isolated for me."

An uneasy silence settled over the group, but Julia diffused the gloom quicky. "Eleven is a lovely age. You must have many exciting adventures ahead of you."

"Indeed. Children bring such merriment and excitement into our lives, don't they?" Emma's gaze lingered on Julia for a moment longer before more memories flooded back into her mind. Happy childhood moments together, and a sad parting. Why, she could be the exact likeness of . . .

William interrupted her thoughts. "Ada, would you like to explore our island? I've been to Rock Island a time or two, and this island is quite different from yours."

Ada's eyes lit up and she smiled. "I would, very much."

William patted her shoulder. "After lunch, then, you can roam 'til your heart's content."

The girl glanced at the long, narrow island and shrugged. There'd be little to explore.

As they headed to the cottage, they came into the shade of the kitchen porch and sat down as the conversation flowed. Small talk stopped when a large freighter passed by, blowing its horn while the sailors waved hello. The ship came surprisingly closer to this island than it would have to Rock Island or as it passed by Thousand Island Park.

As the ship headed west, Michael turned to William.

"We came here to learn more about the tragedy of June seventh—the collision between the steamer and barge. I read about it a little over a month ago, but Lieutenant Worthington suggested I seek your input as to how to improve our rescue techniques for the future, if they are ever needed."

William nodded. "I'd be honored to help in any way I can. Come. There's much to talk about."

While the fellow lightkeepers delved into discussions about the crash, Emma and Ada joined Dee and Julia in the kitchen to help prepare lunch. The small, sunny room just off the porch had large windows for viewing the river. The homey smell of roasting chicken and boiling potatoes welcomed them.

Dee handed Ada a carrot to slice and Emma an onion to dice. "The journey from Rock Island must have been quite a trek. How did you manage?"

To Emma's surprise, Ada responded. "We borrowed a wagon from Papa's friend, drove all the way to Chippewa Bay, and took the skiff from there. It was really far and bumpy, especially to come to a place like this."

Dee chuckled. "Well, glad you made the trip, dear. Say, we grownups can handle things here. Feel free to go out and explore a bit before lunch."

Ada glanced at Emma, and she gave her a nod. "Go ahead, sweetheart."

When the girl fled the cottage, Emma cocked her head, her furrowed brow begging information. "Do you mind me asking, where are you from, Julia?"

"Brockville, in Ontario, Canada. Do you know it?"

The knife slipped from Emma's grasp, producing a sharp clang on the cutting board that reverberated like an alarm. Her hands instinctively covered her mouth as she drew in a deep breath, her eyes widening in astonishment. "I knew it! I just knew it in my bones! You're Myrtle's daughter, aren't you?"

"You knew my mother? How?"

Emma hurried over to Julia and hugged her tightly, her eyes filling. She choked back a sob. "I'm . . . I'm your Aunt Emma. Your mother's sister, though we haven't spoken for a terribly long while. I moved to Thousand Island Park eight years ago, and we . . . well . . . we were disenfranchised for ages."

Dee let out a loud gasp. But then she smiled, motioning toward the inner part of the cottage. "Why don't you two go and talk alone in the parlor? I'll finish up here."

Emma thanked her and followed Julia into the parlor. Her head spun with disbelief. It couldn't be true! How on earth did this happen? And at a lighthouse, no less!

As they settled onto the settee, Julia whimpered,

tears streaming down her cheeks. Clearly, this revelation deeply affected her niece. "My mother always refused to speak of the past. I knew only that she had three sisters, but she wouldn't talk about them. You."

Emma patted her hand. "Oh Julia, I didn't even know you existed, or I'd have made contact. How are your parents?"

Julia groaned, sucked in a deep breath, and sighed. "They died in a boating accident when I was fourteen. Six years ago."

"I'm so sorry for your loss, Julia. I wish I'd known. Our family story is a complicated one that has affected us all. That's probably why your mother didn't want to speak of it. You see, when our parents discovered that our other sister, Lucy, was expecting a child outside of marriage, loyalties splintered and relationships frayed for years. It was a regrettable episode of family foolishness at its worst."

Julia gasped. "What are you talking about?"

Slowly and carefully, Emma told the sad tale of her sister's tragedy. A sailor taking advantage of her. The family sending her away in shame. A baby adopted by another family.

The words hung in the air, the heavy acknowledgment of the relational fractures that time had woven into their family tree. Julia took a deep breath, her eyes meeting Emma's with a blend of sorrow and acceptance.

Emma touched her shoulder, attempting to form a bond with her newfound niece. "There's so much your mother and I never said, so many wounds left to fester in silence. We were separated from one another by circumstances and social bias. I'm so sorry, Julia—for all the wasted years." She placed a comforting hand on Julia's arm, a reminder that they were family. "We can't change the past, dear. But what we can do is face it, acknowledge the pain, and hopefully, forgive. And at least you and I can be family."

Julia nodded. "I want to know the whole truth about my family, even the painful parts. All of it, please. I'm done with secrets."

So was she. For years, the abyss between her family members yawned large, and it hurt. Now, perhaps, she and Julia could begin building their family and heal the pain and isolation of the past. As they talked through their family history, Emma prayed that she could bridge the gap in their family story and be a true aunt to Julia.

But would Julia want that?

Michael enjoyed every bite of their al fresco luncheon on the kitchen's porch. Passing ships, soaring seagulls, and fresh air was just the ticket to revive him after the prior night's stormy vigil, the long journey to the island, and his lack of sleep. Tonight's work would prove a challenge, but he'd been through worse. The past spring had yielded multiple storms where he had to keep the light burning all day and night.

He took a deep breath. Being out on the river always brought him peace. But the tension between Emma and Ada was palpable, and he wasn't sure how to address it in public. Ada constantly drew attention to herself and subtly misbehaved. Just short of needing a scolding. She was a smart little thing. The child knew how to color outside the lines just enough to get away with it, and her charming personality somehow softened her naughtiness.

During lunch, Ada broke every table manner he'd taught her, chewing loudly, clanging her fork on her plate, and slurping her tea. And the mischievous gleam in her eye revealed she was doing it just to spite them. While he tried to address the infractions with pointed looks and subtle shakes of his head, Ada ignored him.

Finally, he'd had enough. He leaned in and whispered, though he knew the others would overhear. "Use your manners, Ada, or you can be excused."

His daughter blinked twice. He had never before scolded her in public. "I'm done. May I be excused to take a walk?"

Not a *please*. No *thank you* for the meal. Just a petulant mood that challenged his authority and reflected poorly on him as a parent.

She'd always been a little moody and sometimes

even obstinate, but this summer, she was twice as challenging. Was it because he married Emma, or was it the normal transition of a girl growing into young womanhood? Maybe both? He had no idea, but he longed for his Ada to become a respectable lady, mother or not. Stepmother or not. His failure as a father or not.

By midafternoon, it was time to head back to Rock Island. The journey would be long and tiring, especially with a grouchy girl. Thankfully, a short way into the wagon ride, Ada fell asleep, so he and Emma were able to talk freely. Still, they kept their voices low, their heads close together so they could hear each other over the crackle of gravel under their wheels and the clop-clop of the horse's hooves.

Emma filled in the details of meeting Julia, and he rejoiced with her. "It's positively providential, I say. What are the chances of that happening? And at a lighthouse. God orchestrates things better than a Bach symphony."

Emma threw back her head and laughed. "And what sweet music it is!"

Suddenly, they hit a pothole, and their heads collided. Hard.

"Ouch!" Emma chuckled as she rubbed her head but continued her tale. "I just can't believe I met my niece. Yes, providence has shined on us today, and I will forever love the young woman with all my heart. Hopefully, they'll all visit us before the summer is out, just as they promised."

He nodded. "And I'd welcome that visit. Anytime. William is a fine chap, and his mother's a delight. But most of all, I'm so happy you found a part of your family, Emma."

Ada stirred. "Not me. That was the boringest day ever. Worse than being alone with you all day, Emma. I'm tired of grownups. When can I go and see Mary?"

Ire prickled the back of his neck. "Ada. Enough! Apologize to Emma at once!"

Ada mumbled "sorry" and stayed silent the rest of the time. Her moodiness was more than he could take sometimes.

By the time they returned to Rock Island, the sun had already dropped low on the horizon, and night was falling fast. He had procrastinated in telling Ada their plans to move Emma into his room—their room—and now it was time.

He hurried to light the porch lamp and was tempted to put off the discussion until the morning. But a promise was a promise.

He took Emma's hand and tugged Ada close with the other. "Ada, before I head to the tower, I want to tell you something. I have decided—*we* have decided—that it's time for Emma to move into my—*our*—room. She's not a guest. She's my wife. So, she'll be sleeping in my—*our*—room from now on."

Ada's eyes narrowed into tiny slits as she pursed

her lips. She pulled away from him. "That's a bad idea, Papa. That's *your* room. Mama should be in there with you, not *her*." The glare she gave Emma could melt an iceberg.

He'd heard enough childishness, and he was tired of it. She'd been cantankerous all day. Disrespectful, even. "Enough, Ada. The decision has been made. Emma will move into our room this very night."

Ada folded her arms over her chest and planted her feet. "It's not fair! I never got to stay in your room 'cept when I was sick. Now *she* gets to? Wife or not, she's a stranger in *my* house."

"Stop it, Ada. Please go to your room and change your mood. I'll see you in the morning."

His daughter's mouth formed a small *o,* but she clamped it shut. She turned and fled the room as guilt enveloped him. He'd never lost his temper with her before. Rarely scolded her. Always gave her the benefit of the doubt, but that was clearly a mistake.

Why did this summer have to be so difficult? They should be forming one big happy family, and he and Emma should be enjoying the romance and joy of being newly married. How had he failed so badly?

He kissed Emma goodnight. Was it too much to wish he could spend one leisurely night in her arms? In the quiet moments before dawn or after Ada had drifted off to sleep, he and Emma had found a few private interludes together in the days past. And though he discovered that intimacy wasn't always about grand gestures or vast expanses of time, he ached for connection and a deepening of their love.

All night long, he fretted and allowed his thoughts to fester like an infected boil. And he was tired. Grouchy.

As the first light of dawn signaled his long, exhausted evening of keeping the light was coming to an end, he chided himself. He was a failure as a husband and a father. He was culpable for his family's discomfort. He'd chosen a job that kept him up all night and isolated them from others.

And though he had thought it was for the best for Ada, he'd sent her away to school hoping to provide her with the education, friends, and the future he wanted for her. Apparently, she hadn't learned to be kind, considerate, and accommodating. But worst of all, he married Emma without bothering to ask his daughter's thoughts on the matter or prepare her better. Now, both Emma and Ada were hurting.

His failure enveloped him like a heavy fog, and he had no idea how to vanquish it. Somehow, he had to be the father his daughter needed, but would that keep Emma away? His first responsibility was to his wife, but besides his mother, he was all Ada had. How could he facilitate the essential peace between Ada and Emma?

When dawn finally came, Michael extinguished the light, set everything in order, and descended the ladder and then the spiral staircase. He visited the tiny privy and returned to the cottage, hoping Emma was up and ready to lend him some counsel.

The comforting smell of coffee wafted through the screen door, welcoming him into his home. He loved it here, and he hoped Emma and Ada did too. Perhaps that, too, was a failure on his part.

"Good morning, my sweet husband. How did you do with no sleep?" Emma's cheery voice enveloped him with love.

"Hello, my dear." He kissed her softly and sat down, exhausted physically and emotionally.

Emma poured him a cup of steaming coffee and set it before him. She smoothed his hair and wrapped her arms around his shoulders. "I had planned on joining you for a while last night, knowing how tired you must have been. I must have fallen asleep and just woke up a little while ago."

He tilted his head, laying his cheek on her hand. "Thanks for thinking of me, darling. I probably wouldn't have been very good company. Ada's sullenness is getting to me, and I'm not sure what to do."

Emma kissed his cheek and sat next to him.

"She's testing us both, but you were right to be strong with her last night. She has to know her boundaries and not be allowed to stomp over them."

"You're right, of course. But she's very good at stepping a toenail just over the line so she gets away with it, as she did yesterday."

Emma shrugged. "Then we'll just have to keep her toenails trimmed."

Despite his exhaustion and worries, Michael laughed long and loud, grateful for a respite of humor he so desperately needed.

Chapter 9

Three days later, after arriving at Thousand Island Park and dropping Ada to play with Mary, Emma sent Michael off to spend time with Mr. Wiseman while she visited with her best friend. She'd been itching to see her for days.

Laurie Jean welcomed Emma inside her lovely cottage trimmed in lavender. An array of doilies sat underneath a plethora of knickknacks. She led Emma to the table where a steaming pot of tea and blueberry scones awaited her arrival.

Emma sat at the table and grinned. "This looks wonderful, my friend. How are you?"

Her friend was a few years older and had been married for more than two decades. She had three children, already grown and married, and her wisdom was bottomless. Her blond hair and crystal-blue eyes hinted at her Scandinavian heritage.

Laurie Jean poured the tea. "I'm fine as the flowers blooming in my garden, and the family is well. My son saw you coming this way and alerted me, so I put on the kettle, and I'm grateful I had two fresh scones leftover from breakfast."

"Thank you, but tell me your latest news, please."

"Robert and I just celebrated our twenty-second

anniversary, but nothing else is new. Besides, I want to hear all about *your* new life and the many changes. Tell all, girl."

Emma bit her bottom lip, wondering what to say. She didn't want to disparage her husband. He was a wonderful man, loving, kind, generous, and a faithful servant. But Ada—and the way Michael avoided disciplining her—was another story.

She took a deep breath and sought Laurie Jean's counsel. "Being married to Michael is a gift from God, and I wouldn't change that for the world. But I don't know how to be the stepmother Ada needs."

Laurie Jean set down her teacup and took one of Emma's hands. "First thing, get rid of the word *step*. You're her mother now, and though you can never replace her birth mother or the memory of her—nor would you—you need to be confident in your role. Children can smell fear or uncertainty a mile away."

She chuckled. "More than you know, and Ada has the nose for it, especially where her father is concerned."

Laurie Jean's cocked head questioned her. "What do you mean?"

"Michael tends to overlook the smaller infractions and avoid confrontation with his daughter. I want to be a caring and loving presence in Ada's life, but it feels as though I'm an outsider, navigating uncharted waters, and I fear I'll crash into an emotional shoal at any moment."

Her friend nodded. "I've felt that way, too, even with my own children, especially Stevie. But it's more complicated in your situation. Ada and Michael have been a team for four years now. Letting you into their tiny circle might be threatening to the girl, and she being an only child, at that." Laurie Jean paused and took a sip of tea before continuing. "Remember that Rome wasn't built in a day. These things take time. Build your relationships with love, care, and lots of patience for them and for you. It's a delicate dance, my dear friend. And pray. Don't forget to ask God to help you."

Emma frowned. She'd prayed a few times, but in the heat of the moment, she often forgot that He knew best what was needed. "That's so true. I need to mend my ways in that regard."

Laurie Jean poured them both some more tea. "You've had a blizzard of change thrust upon you, so don't be too hard on yourself. God will guide you on this journey. It's just a matter of finding that balance between being a wife and mother—not *stepmother*—while building peace and harmony into your new family. The Cinderella story really did do a disservice to women such as you who take on that vital role, and I applaud you, Emma."

"Thanks, though I'm not sure applause is deserved."

Laurie Jean shrugged, patting her hand before taking a bite of her scone. The several moments of silence was deafening. Did she agree that Emma didn't deserve such praise? It was all so confusing, and she didn't know what to say.

To her relief, her friend continued. "Not every woman would take on a child who is heading into womanhood and assume a position such as a lightkeeper's wife. I know there are a lot of sacrifices in that particular role. But everything is an opportunity for growth and learning. And remember to take time for yourself and your relationship with your Maker. He can show you what to do and give you the strength to do it."

"It's comforting to have a dear friend like you to confide in, who knows how to help. I feel better already."

"Good. Now then, how are you finding married life?" A wide grin and twinkle in her eyes hinted that she spoke of intimacy.

That, however, was a topic Emma would keep to herself. She flushed at the delight she'd shared in the secret rendezvous around the island with her husband. "Michael's a dear. He's not much of a talker, but he works hard and affirms me every day. He calls me the most endearing names. Those are priceless gifts for which I'm grateful. I just wish . . ."

"Wish what, my friend?" Laurie Jean's raised brows.

"I feel as though I'm constantly walking on eggshells when it comes to Michael and his daughter. I worry about interfering where I don't belong, especially when he avoids disciplining her. One minute I feel like an outsider. The next I want to take the bull by the horns and deal with issues he overlooks."

Laurie Jean exhaled heavily. "I've felt that way too. I was always the disciplinarian. Robert avoided it like a summer sunburn. Have you talked with Michael about your distress?"

"I have, but he thinks I don't understand because I'm not a mother, and he dismisses Ada's disrespect and belligerence as childish mischief. I'm torn between wanting to create a loving home and feeling as though I don't belong there. I don't want to criticize Ada or Michael's parenting choices, but . . ."

With that, she clamped her hand over her mouth. She'd said too much. Something she vowed never to do. Guilt and regret soured her stomach and pained her heart.

Laurie Jean nodded. "Oh, my friend. You're not alone. It was the same with me. Robert avoided anything resembling confrontation, and the kids knew it. But keep on communicating. Sooner or later, he'll understand. And please, give yourself—and them—lots of mercy."

Emma took a sip of her tea. "I'll try. Thanks for listening."

Laurie Jean set her napkin on the table and stood. "Let's take a walk and find our way to the Columbian for lunch with your husband. Shall we?"

"Yes, let's!" Grateful the difficult conversation had ended, Emma joined her in clearing the table and washing the dishes. Then they strolled down Rainbow Avenue to Coast Avenue along the shoreline. The midday sun was warm, but the breeze off the river was refreshing.

So was the company. They stopped to greet many of their neighbors and friends she missed. When she married, she knew that life would be different, but people were who she missed the most. Every encounter on her walk filled her with joy.

When they got to St. Lawrence Avenue, they headed straight for the small stone library where she'd worked for eight wonderful years. Before they entered, Laurie Jean gave her a warning. "Mrs. Potter is our temporary librarian. We still haven't found your replacement."

Emma groaned, dismay ticking her pulse up a bit. "But she can't tolerate children a whit."

"And that's why she's temporary."

They entered the building and stopped. Piles of books waited to be shelved, and Mrs. Potter slumped over, sleeping at her desk. A few patrons sat reading, but the one-room library was quiet. Emma's heart clenched. Oh, how she loved it here. The soothing smell of books. The familiar creak of the floor. The old scarred desk.

She cleared her throat. "Good day to you, missus."

A loud snort came from the old woman, and when she raised her head, drool ran down her chin. She wiped it away. "Good day to you, Emma. Laurie Jean."

Emma ached to shelve the books. "How's the library treating you?"

Mrs. Potter groaned loudly. "I'm too old for this, especially when the young 'uns show up. Hope they'll find someone soon."

Emma smiled warmly. "Would you like me to shelve the books for you? I'd be happy to help."

Mrs. Potter's face lit up as though she'd seen Santa Claus. "I'm be much obliged, dear. My rheumatism is acting up somethin' fierce these days. It's hard to even get these old bones here to open the library anymore. Can't be doing this much longer."

Laurie Jean picked up a pile of books. "That's understandable. I'll help Emma, and we'll have these shelved in two shakes of a lamb's tail."

The old woman let out a sigh as a patron entered. She didn't greet the mother and child. Instead, she scowled. "Keep that child tight in your grip, ma'am. I can't be having no monkey business in my library."

Emma's pulse quickened with ire. She always

welcomed children to *her* library. As far as she was concerned, a kind librarian made good readers. She had loved doing story time with the children every Monday morning and Friday afternoon. She'd read the stories with funny voices and lots of inflection, and the children loved it. And once a month, she did a craft with them too. They loved her, and she them.

Truth was, she missed her life here. Her simple, busy life. Had she made a mistake in marrying so quickly and Michael in not preparing Ada for the changes to come?

Michael tamped down his frustration as he made his way to the Columbian Hotel, hoping Mr. Wiseman sat in his usual spot at the chessboard table on the veranda. The retired preacher could offer him some sound counsel and support—of that, he was sure.

Thankfully, Mr. Wiseman sat people watching, as was his custom. Michael waved, and the elderly gentleman slowly stood, a hearty grin of welcome on his wrinkled face. Like everyone in the community, Michael loved him, respected his wealth of wisdom, and needed to tap into it.

He climbed the steps to the veranda and made his way to the corner where Mr. Wiseman waited. Michael put out his hand. "Good morning, sir. And how are you on this fine July morning?"

Mr. Wiseman shook it. "Rejoicing in the

Creator's beauty and grateful to see my light-keeping friend, that's what. Shall we partake in a game of chess while we catch up?"

Michael chuckled. "Let's, but I can't hope to beat you."

The older man shrugged as he sat and soon moved his pawn. "No matter. It's just to pass the time as we visit. How's married life and fatherhood? I'm guessing there are a few changes and challenges, so I've been praying for you. For all three of you."

Praying for them? Michael wasn't much of a praying man, especially since God took his wife so tragically. Perhaps he should change that. He moved a pawn two spaces. "Thank you. It's been, well, interesting. Emma is a dear—patient, kind. The perfect wife and mother. But Ada has been—how should I say?—difficult."

Mr. Wiseman guffawed. "I can imagine. She's been a crackerjack since she was a wee thing. I remember her trying your patience during Sunday services when she was barely out of diapers. And since she's been away at boarding school, she seems to have grown even more—er—independent."

His friend saw his daughter's willfulness too. Did everyone? "Yes. It's true. But this year seems the worst."

The elderly man moved a rook one space. "She's on her way to womanhood, Michael. My daughter was impossible during those changing years. But Ada has added challenges—the loss of a mother and a new mother."

"But that's the point. Emma is a wonderful woman. She treats Ada with more love and gentleness than she sometimes deserves. Why can't Ada just accept her?"

Mr. Wiseman rubbed his chin. "I'm sorry we didn't speak about this earlier. It crossed my mind, but then the wedding happened so fast, we didn't have a chance to talk. I regret that. My theory is that Ada is likely jealous that she has to share you with Emma. She's probably also conflicted in her loyalties—her allegiance to her mother or to Emma."

Michael had thought the same. "I feel so guilty. I constantly question if I'm doing the right thing for her and for Emma. I'm caught between my support for Ada and my commitment to Emma. I want to build a strong foundation for my family, but I don't know how."

Mr. Wiseman moved his rook and took one of Michael's pawns. He shook it at Michael before placing it to the side. "Have you talked with them about your worries?"

He sighed. "You know I'm not much of a talker. I'm more of a doer. I don't want to burden them or make them feel responsible for my feelings or failures."

"Rubbish. Open communication is crucial,

Michael. All three of you are making huge adjustments in life, and you have to learn to understand each other. Emma and Ada might be feeling the same way or have concerns of their own. Don't sweep any of it under the rug, Michael. Discuss it."

A long silence ensued as the old man seemed to study his next move. Michael braced himself for a big play. But then, his mentor simply moved a pawn one space. "May I be frank, Michael?"

Oh no! The man had been a preacher for decades and counseled folks all his life. The word *frank* meant that a reprimand followed. "Certainly, sir."

Mr. Wiseman cleared his throat and leaned in. "You know I'm a people watcher, and I've watched you through the years. You adore your daughter, as you should, but sometimes, I think you're blind to her manipulative behavior. I've seen her wrap you around her little finger and tug you into submission. She's become quite adept at it, Michael, and I fear it might be her downfall if you don't change things."

Could he be right? He took one of Mr. Wiseman's pawns. One tiny victory.

If he were honest, he knew it was true. "What do I do, then?"

"Establish clear boundaries and expectations, and never let her cross the line. But also foster your relationship with her and with Emma—and with all three of you together. I admit that you have your work cut out for you, son, but you can do it, with God's help."

Michael's stomach churned at the realization he had let them down. Failed at being a good father. Failed at being a new husband. "Perhaps, in hindsight, a year alone with Emma would have helped."

The old man shrugged as he slid his bishop several spaces and took a knight. "Perhaps. Or perhaps Ada would've seen the marriage as abandonment, or as replacing her, and she'd never forgive you. Let the 'what ifs' go, sir, and deal with 'what is' today. Be patient with yourself and forgive the past. And pray for wisdom. Pray that God will give you understanding. Move forward, and celebrate the good things that happen." He paused and moved his rook. "Unfortunately, my friend, I'm sorry to say that this moment is not one of them. Checkmate!"

Michael scanned the board to find he, indeed, was beat. He tipped his king down and grinned. "Has anyone ever beat you, sir?"

Mr. Wiseman chuckled. "A few. A very few."

"Hello, gentlemen. Anyone hungry?" Emma and Laurie Jean waved as they climbed the hotel steps and joined them. Emma giggled. "He beat you again, husband?"

Michael took her hand and squeezed it. "Always. Will you join us for luncheon, sir? Our treat."

Slowly, Mr. Wiseman stood. "Thank you. Hello, Emma and Laurie Jean. And how are you lovely ladies on this fine day?"

They both said, "wonderful" at the same time and laughed. Laurie Jean held Mr. Wiseman's arm, and Emma slipped her hand into the crook of Michael's as they headed inside.

When they took their seats in the dining room, a flood of sweet memories entered his thoughts. Memories of unhindered luncheons with Emma—before they married. Everything was easier before they married.

Had they made a terrible mistake?

"Goodness! I've had an idea. See what you think . . ." Emma turned to her friend, excitement radiating from her as she sat up straight. "I think you should be the new librarian, Laurie Jean. You'd be perfect. Your children are grown, and you love kids. You love books too."

Laurie Jean's eyes lit up. "Really? I do have too much time on my hands these days. Perhaps I'll speak to Robert about it. Thanks for the idea, Emma."

As a waiter arrived at their table, Michael took Emma's hand and squeezed it. "That's a capital notion. My wife is chock full of ideas, isn't she? Shall we order?"

During the meal, none of them mentioned Ada or the challenges marriage brought. Thank heavens. Instead, they spoke about the latest events around the Park, who was coming to sing or teach or preach, and village scuttlebutt.

Michael couldn't fail to notice that Emma listened to every tidbit with rapt attention. Did she regret not being here, not being a part of the excitement? Did she wish she'd not married and chained herself to a husband, child, and island? Was God truly at work in their lives, in their marriage?

The more he thought about it, the sadder he became. Perhaps he should let her stay . . .

As Emma related in detail the story of finding Julia at Sister Island, Michael thought about the last four years of his life. He'd ignored God. If he'd admit it, he was angry with Him for leaving him to father Ada alone, for hurting his child, for leaving him without his wife. For ruining his happily ever after. He didn't *not* believe. He didn't reject God. He just . . . well, ignored Him.

"What do you think, Michael?" Mr. Wiseman was addressing him, and he'd been ignoring them, lost in his thoughts. He couldn't even hold up the social front he once could. Was he falling down in every area of life?

He blinked. "Sorry. What were you asking?"

"Would you like to join us for the church picnic this Sunday? There will be a choir and games and watermelon. What do you say?"

How could he say no? But what if the rest of the community caught wind of his failures as a husband and father? They loved Emma. Would support her, no matter what. Could he risk being found out? Still, Emma's hopeful smile prodded him to accept.

"We'd love to join you, friends."

Chapter 10

As Emma prepared for Sunday services, she worried about the possibility of Ada making a scene. Ever since she'd spent the day with Mary, the child had grumbled and fought her at every turn. For five long days, she'd refused to help with chores, and Michael had dismissed it, claiming that she wasn't used to work. When Michael wasn't nearby, the girl had huffed her displeasure, saying, "My mother never made me be a slave."

Ada had even put extra salt in the soup, feigning innocence and accusing Emma of being a bad cook. And though Michael ate it, she knew he knew and was simply avoiding confrontation.

Perhaps church and a day away would settle her frayed nerves. And she prayed Ada would turn a corner soon.

Still in the bedroom while the others waited below, Emma fixed her hair and grabbed her bonnet. But the strings had been tied in tight knots. Ada. She fumed as she struggled to untie them.

"Emma. Come. We'll be late for service." Michael's voice from the foyer carried a tinge of exasperation.

Well, she was just as exasperated! "Coming.

Someone tied knots in my bonnet strings."

When she reached for her gloves, they were missing. She had left them where she always did, safe and secure in the top drawer.

They'd be late for service, all right, and it was Ada's doing. She stomped down the stairs, tired of playing the endless games. "Where are my gloves, Ada?"

Ada slipped her hand into her father's. "Why do you always accuse me of things? They're *your* gloves."

Michael sighed. "Let's go without them, Emma. No need to be late for church over a pair of gloves."

Emma placed her hands on her hips. "Where are they, Ada?"

The child shrugged. "I might have seen them behind the chair in the parlor."

Emma quickly retrieved them and the picnic basket, donning the gloves as they walked to the boat. Despite the sunny day and puffy clouds, the morning felt stormy. Dealing with a disrespectful girl was one thing. Not being supported by your husband was another.

Michael let go of Ada's hand as she got into the boat. "You need to stop these pranks, darling."

The girl was not a darling. Emma had heard enough. "They're not pranks, Michael. Ada, you need to leave my things alone."

Ada pouted. "You blame me for everything.

You hate me. I bet you wished I wasn't even here."

"I don't hate you, Ada. I love you. But your disrespect and disobedience are not harmless pranks. They hurt." Her voice sounded small, shaky, as it did when she was about to cry. She swallowed the lump in her throat and held her tongue.

Michael stared at her as he pushed off the dock and rowed toward Thousand Island Park. "I'm sorry, Emma. Perhaps we should set all this aside and enjoy the Lord's day."

Could he really be chiding her in front of his daughter? Dismay made her skin crawl and her hair prickle. Her husband willingly, knowingly chose to support his daughter's disrespect over his wife?

Her eyes narrowed, but she pasted her lips together tightly. She refused to confront her husband in front of his daughter. That would be just as disrespectful.

But her heart ached with feelings of being abandoned and dishonored, and though she took his arm as he escorted her into the church, she felt no comfort from it. Instead, she felt a fraud.

The minister spoke on Matthew 7:12—to do to others what you'd have them do to you. She glanced at Ada, who leafed through the pages of her hymnal. She prayed the girl was listening.

Pastor concluded, "Respect is not a passive

virtue but an active choice we make every day. As followers of Christ, we are called to embody respect in our thoughts, words, and actions. May we be known as a community that reflects the love and respect of our Lord and each other, transforming lives and shining the light of hope in a divided world."

How about respect in a divided home?

When service finished, many well-wishers who had been at the wedding or heard of their union came up to them, patting Michael on the back and congratulating them. Emma kept her composure through it all, relieved that Ada had made a quick exit to be with Mary.

Good riddance! They both needed some space from one another. Besides, the adulation would likely have caused more furor in the child.

What was she going to do? Without Michael's backing, she was alone. Very alone.

When they exited the church, Robert joined them and clapped Michael on the back. "You're joining us for the picnic, right? I'd love to catch up. Laurie Jean hurried home to grab the food."

Michael glanced at Emma, a touch of sadness—or was it uncertainty?—in his eyes. "We're looking forward to it, aren't we, Emma?"

She nodded, but their relational temperature was about twenty below zero.

Ada ran to her father with Mary in tow. "Can I please eat with Mary, Papa? Please?"

Michael smiled. "Of course, darling. If it's okay with her aunts."

Mary clapped her hands. "They invited her, sir. Thank you."

The girls ran off to picnic with Mary's aunts. Relief washed over Emma. At least she'd be free of Ada's cheek for a little while.

She shouldn't feel that way. Didn't want to feel that way. But she did. The girl was like a pebble in her shoe, unsettling her at every turn. That, however, wasn't the worst of it. Feeling abandoned by her husband hurt even more.

They found a grassy spot, and she spread her quilt just as Laurie Jean joined them. The men sat down, opening the picnic baskets with eager smiles.

"Have you heard from Julia, Emma?" Laurie Jean smiled at her. It took a moment to realize what she'd asked.

Emma tucked a stray curl behind her ear. "She sent a letter just this week. She and the Dodges will come for Sunday lunch in two weeks. It'll be wonderful to see her again." Her voice held no excitement, no joy. Laurie Jean must've noticed.

Before she sat, Laurie Jean grabbed her hand. "I need to stretch my legs. Will you walk with me, Emma?"

Emma glanced at the men, who were deep in conversation about Robert's latest fishing expedition. "I'll be back soon, Michael. Laurie Jean and I are going to take a walk."

Michael waved her off. "Have fun, but don't be surprised if we eat all the fried chicken while you're gone."

Robert chuckled. "Don't worry. We'll save you a piece or two, ladies."

When they were out of earshot, Laurie Jean squeezed her arm and leaned close. "I know that look. What's eating you?"

They walked along the quiet road, where thankfully, there were no nosy busybodies to hear them. Should she reveal her angst? She didn't want to disparage her husband—or his daughter. But she was so frustrated. "Ada seems determined to make my life miserable, and Michael still brushes it off as if her actions are of no consequence."

Laurie Jean frowned. "Nothing's changed?"

"It's gotten worse, and I don't know what to do."

Her friend squeezed her arm. "Give it time, Emma. Ada will come around."

Laurie Jean didn't support her either?

"How much time? How many pranks and naughtiness and disrespect must I endure before Michael takes this seriously?"

Her friend slipped her arm into the crook of hers, helping her feel accepted. Loved. "He's probably clueless, and she's testing you. Stay strong. Be patient. Keep on praying and showing her love, even when it's hard. Prove that you're here to stay, no matter what."

Emma glanced at the picnic grounds to where Ada was laughing and playing with Mary and a few other children. Gone was the sullen child. She looked free. Happy. As a girl should be.

"Pray for me, please. I need to be strong to win Ada's trust and affection, and I'm not sure I'm up for the task."

Laurie Jean patted her hand. "You are. Trust God to give you strength. Your husband will come around too. He's a good man."

"He is a good man, and I'm blessed to be his wife."

With that, she and Laurie Jean strolled back through the crowd of picnickers. As they passed by, they heard old Mrs. Bradley mention Emma's name to her neighbor, Mrs. Chester. Both had their backs to them, so they slowed to listen.

"Emma doesn't know a whit about childrearing. And that child has spent too much time in the city with too little supervision. She's wild and her tongue is unhinged, I say, and Emma hasn't a clue how to manage her."

Exchanging an indignant glance, Laurie Jean and Emma honed in to hear more.

Mrs. Chester *tsk*ed. "She doesn't, but Mr. Diepolder has been far too lenient with the girl. That's why she's wild."

Emma's stomach clenched. Be it a motherly instinct or just supporting someone who was being defamed, her heart ached for both Michael and Ada. How dare they speak ill of them. A lump filled her throat and tears her eyes. "They have no right to judge."

Laurie Jean tugged her forward. "No, they don't, and it's none of their business. Unfortunately, those two tend to have judgments about everything. Wait until it's their turn. The ninth commandment says, 'You shall not bear false witness against your neighbor.' They'll have a few words to account for when they meet their maker. Let Him be the judge of them, my friend."

"You're right, of course, but it still hurts. I feel so helpless and misunderstood. And alone."

Laurie Jean reached over and hugged her tightly. "You're never alone, Emma. God is with you. He will help you find your way. Trust Him. And know that I'm just across the river."

Her friend was right. She should trust God to get her through everything. But what would it take to change things? A tragedy? Her failed marriage?

Michael was tired. Tired of the incessant tension. Tired of the bickering. Tired of being caught in the middle of the two people he loved most.

The afternoon sun dipped low as he rowed them back to Rock Island, the world seeming peaceful in the deepening shadows. But that peace wouldn't last.

Just then, Ada leaned in and poked the side of

Emma's hat. "That bonnet looks as though it was left over from the Civil War, Emma. Don't you have a hat that's more modern? No one in the city would be caught dead in something like that, and my friends here think you look like an old maid." Her words dripped with condescension.

Michael stopped rowing. "Ada!"

Emma frowned, and her face flushed with a clear mix of anger and embarrassment. She glared at him and bit her lip, silently pleading with him to intervene and defend her. She'd worn that bonnet with pride, a treasured heirloom from her mother, as she'd told him the day after they wed. He should scold Ada. Defend Emma.

But what was a man to do? He only saw Ada during the summer recess and at Christmas—though that was his fault too. Why should he rock the boat during the few precious weeks they had together? Better to keep the peace and enjoy the little time they had left before she went back to school.

Yet Emma was his bride, and she was hurting because of his daughter. Emma had given him that same helpless, distressed look a dozen times, but he never knew what to say.

He'd always been a man of few words, more comfortable with the solitude of a quiet night in the lighthouse than with two bickering women or engaging in testy confrontations. Now, caught between his wife's pain and his daughter's sharp tongue, he felt like a helpless rabbit trapped between two cunning foxes.

Emma continued to stare at him, her eyes brimming with tears as she urged him to help, but his mind went blank. Words failed him, as they often did, leaving him feeling frustrated and inadequate. He loved Emma and hated seeing her hurt, but he couldn't find the right words to defend her or to discipline his daughter without the risk of alienating Ada, perhaps permanently.

Finally, he mustered the courage to speak up. "Ada, you need to keep your opinions to yourself, and Emma, my dear, your worth extends far beyond your bonnet."

Ada blinked as if realizing her thoughtlessness. Her face scrunched up, and she shifted in her seat. "I didn't mean anything by that, Emma. Sorry."

Michael beamed. He'd diffused the situation. A small victory, but he'd take it.

Emma took a deep breath, and a glimmer of relief washed over her pretty face. She really was a beauty, inside and out. "Thank you, Michael, and thank you, Ada. Let's put this behind us."

But her eyes still glittered with hurt. Pain. Disappointment.

By the time they arrived at the island and disembarked the skiff, Ada wanted to spend some time with Midnight, so he and Emma took a few moments to stroll the island alone.

Michael had sensed a shift in Emma's demeanor, a subtle change that he had slowly come to recognize over the past month. The way her brow furrowed slightly, the way her gaze seemed to drift off into the distance. And when they visited Thousand Island Park, her wistful sadness shook him. All these were tell-tale signs that she was wrestling with something deep. But what was it, and what could he do about it?

As they walked along the shore, he reached out and gently took her hand, his callused fingers intertwining with hers. "Emma, my love, is everything alright?"

Emma hesitated for a moment. She seemed to be unsure of how to articulate the tumultuous thoughts swirling in her eyes. "I . . ." she began, her voice barely above a whisper. "I'm not sure, Michael. I can't help but wonder if I made the right choice in leaving everything behind—my job, my home, my old life."

His heart sank at her words. He had known that the transition would not be an easy one, but he'd hoped that she would have found the same peace and fulfillment he had discovered on the island. The thought that his beloved wife might be second-guessing her decision shattered his tenuous sense of security.

"Emma, my darling, what is it that troubles you? I know you and Ada have had some struggles, but . . ." His grip on her hand tightened ever so slightly. "Is it Ada? Or something else?"

She sighed, her gaze fixed on the shoreline. "It's not just Ada, Michael. It's . . . everything. The isolation, missing my friends, the challenges of being a stepmother. Some days, I find myself longing for the familiarity of Thousand Island Park, the bustle of the library, the sense of belonging I once had. Here, I feel like I'm an outsider, and I feel like I'm failing you and Ada on every front."

The tightening noose of guilt and uncertainty threatened to suffocate him. Had he been so blinded by his love for Emma that he had failed to see the toll this new life was taking on her? He had thought that his devotion, his support, and the beauty of the island would be enough to sustain her, but he may have been sorely mistaken.

"Emma, you're not an outsider, and you're not failing us. I . . . I had no idea you were struggling so much." As the words left his lips, a deep sense of vulnerability stirred. The fear of Emma leaving him, of returning to her old life without him, was a prospect he had never truly considered.

She stopped and looked deep into his eyes, imploring him. "I know the importance of your work, Michael, and your devotion to your daughter is commendable. But as your wife, sleeping alone night after night while you tend to the light is harder than I imagined, and though I know you need your rest, when morning comes, you sleep away the hours while Ada and I bicker. I just didn't realize how difficult all this would be. When can we find time for us, especially with Ada in the house?"

He frowned. "I know finding moments of intimacy and connection is important, love, but my work and Ada are important too."

"I realize that, but when will we have unhindered time together?"

"Once Ada is back in school, we will."

Emma groaned.

Michael grimaced. He'd just suggested that they'd have to wait to be alone until the fall. What a dunderhead!

"I'm so sorry, Emma. I didn't mean that." A tiny huff escaped his lips. "I share your frustration, truly, but you knew Ada would be here with us when you agreed to marry me. Love often requires compromise and creativity, and when a child is present, that's often the case. Yet, even though we may not have consistent privacy right now, we can still enjoy our stolen moments, can't we?"

Tears welled up in her eyes and ran down her cheeks. "Have we made a terrible mistake marrying so quickly? I miss the life I left behind—the cozy library, the familiar faces of colleagues and friends, the sense of security and routine I had taken for granted. I feel like I'm caught in a tug-of-war between the life I've chosen and the life I left behind. I love you, Michael, with every fiber of my being, but the responsibility of being a stepmother to Ada is so overwhelming."

Michael swallowed the lump choking him. "The truth is, I've failed you, my precious wife, and I'm so sorry. I've tried my best to be both mother and father to Ada for so long that I've been blind to your needs. But I can't be the lightkeeper this community depends on, the present, engaged father Ada needs, and the husband you deserve. I don't know what to do either." Tears welled up in his eyes as he spoke, his love for Emma intertwining with his sense of inadequacy.

For several moments, they stood on the shore, silently warring within themselves. But then, Emma whispered, "No! Giving up on this marriage, on this family, is not an option. Ever! It would be the ultimate betrayal, not only to you and to Ada, but also to the God I serve."

Michael pulled her into a tight embrace and kissed her temple. "I agree, my darling wife. We'll make it through these tough times together."

She sniffled and blew out a deep breath. "We must."

But a nagging fear took root in the back of his mind. What if it took a tragedy, some profound loss, to finally secure their bonds as a family?

The very idea caused a shiver to run down his spine.

Chapter 11

On a sunny Sunday morning two weeks later, Emma set down her fork and scanned Julia's letter again. "Julia and the Dodges should be here for the noon meal."

Michael nodded, turning to Ada. "Guess I'd better take you to Fishers Landing to see your friend, Elsa, and then I'll catch a few winks before they get here. I'm pretty tired. That fog last night had me on pins and needles, but thankfully, it passed without incident."

Ada pushed her eggs around her plate. "I'm not hungry, and I'm ready to go, Papa. Emma likes Julia more than me, so I don't want to be here."

Emma sucked in a breath. "She's my niece, but I only met her that once. We're family, Ada, and you're my daughter."

"Stepdaughter. Like Cinderella."

Emma shook her head—and her forefinger. "No! Not like Cinderella. That's a sad story from the sixteen hundreds, but we are nothing like that. I love you, Ada, more than you know."

Michael agreed. "She loves you, sweetheart. We both do."

Truth be told, Emma was choosing to love Ada. In the past two weeks, she'd endured days of Ada playfully tilting the picture frames in the parlor, causing Emma to repeatedly straighten them. When confronted, a cheeky grin and wide eyes were the child's only response. A subtle prank, but annoying, still.

Ada had even caught Emma and Michael in a little tryst in his workshop and made a terrible ruckus about it for days.

And though Emma carefully established rules for cleaning up after herself, Ada refused. She consistently left her books, shoes, and toys around. Just two days ago, Emma tripped over a boot Ada left in the kitchen doorway, spilling hot tea and breaking a fine china teacup. When confronted, Ada screamed, stomped her foot, and blamed her. "You broke my mother's favorite teacup. You must hate us both!"

Michael pulled himself out of bed when he heard the disturbance that morning. But after calming Ada down and discovering what had happened, he brushed it all off as a mere accident—on both of their counts.

After that, he returned to bed, but Emma wasn't finished with Ada. "These pranks you've been pulling aren't right, and this behavior is unacceptable. We need to build a respectful relationship."

Instead of apologizing, Ada had feigned not feeling well, rubbing her neck. "My throat is scratchy. Can I go out and get some fresh air now?"

Emma had waved her out the door, but her frustration only grew. Though Laurie Jean had counseled that the girl's pranks stemmed from wanting acceptance and reassurance that Emma would never leave, waiting for her to realize that was no easy task.

"Ready, darlin'?" Michael cut into her thoughts as he stood and took Ada's hand. He turned to Emma, planting a quick kiss on her cheek. "I'll be back shortly, love."

After they left, she sat sipping her tea, fingering her spectacles and pondering her challenges. Yes, she and Ada had enjoyed a few pleasant moments cooking together and several more talking about books and science. They even took a walk around the island and engaged in a heartfelt conversation about nature. But more often than not, pranks, mischief, and condescending remarks tainted their days. Without Michael's discipline, that was unlikely to change.

"Ah, well, enough sadness. Julia and the Dodges will be here soon." She laughed as she realized she'd spoken her thoughts aloud. To no one.

Michael returned within the hour, and another hour or more passed with him sleeping. Emma busied herself preparing the noon meal, and before long, the morning had flown by.

A knock at the front door alerted her that guests had arrived. Instead, their former pastor stood there. The older man had thick white hair, tiny round spectacles, and a large paunch. If he grew a beard, he could pass for Santa.

"Goodness! Pastor Cantwell. Welcome. Please come in, and I'll get you some tea." What was he doing here?

"Welcome, Pastor." Michael appeared, bleary-eyed but with a smile on his face. "Goodness! I forgot you were coming today. But please, stay for dinner."

Michael cast her an apologetic grin. She gave him a reassuring nod. She'd made plenty of food, and the man was always welcome at their table.

Soon a small steamer docked. Excitement coursed through her veins when she confirmed it was Julia and the Dodges. She stepped onto the porch and waved, calling out to them, "Welcome! I hope you're hungry. Dinner is almost ready."

Julia smiled at her but continued chatting with the Dodges on her way to the cottage. She wore a soft yellow dress and matching bonnet. Pretty as a spring daffodil, she was. As they climbed the porch steps, William squeezed Julia's hand.

Were they a couple? Wouldn't that be lovely?

Emma hugged each of them, welcoming them onto the island. "You're right on time. I've been cooking up a storm to celebrate your visit."

Julia held onto her embrace an extra moment or two. "It's so good to see you again, Aunt Emma!"

Emma guided them into the parlor, where Michael and Pastor Cantwell sat playing checkers. "This is Pastor Cantwell from Fineview, just down the road from Thousand Island Park where he was pastor for years. I hope you don't mind him joining us for this family dinner."

William shook his hand. "On the contrary. We're honored. Pleased to meet you, sir."

Michael stood and introduced them. "This is the Sister Island lightkeeper, William Dodge and his mother, Mrs. Dodge. And this is our niece, Miss Julia Collins, from Brockville, Ontario, Canada."

Julia and Dee curtsied, and Pastor Cantwell acknowledged them before shaking William's hand. "Good to know you, folks. Thanks for allowing this old bachelor to join you. It isn't often I get a delectable home-cooked meal these days."

Dee chuckled. "Well, you're welcome to come up to Sister Island for a home-cooked meal anytime, sir. We'd love a visit from a man of the cloth. And our family tradition is much the same as here. The first time, you're company. After that, you're family."

Pastor Cantwell guffawed. "I'll remember that, but it's a far piece up there, isn't it?"

William nodded. "An hour or so by steamer, if you rent or catch a ride on one. Otherwise, it's a few hours by land and a quick skiff ride to the island."

Michael gestured to the comfortable chairs and

invited everyone to make themselves at home. "It's a full day's travel either way, but you'd come home with a contented belly and a light heart. I can guarantee that."

Emma excused herself and returned with a tray of freshly baked biscuits, which she set on the table. "I thought we could start with these while the potatoes finish boiling."

Julia took a biscuit, licking her lips at the succulent and buttery goodness. "These are heavenly, Aunt Emma. Thank you. But where's Ada?"

Emma's cheeks warmed at the compliment. "Thank you, niece. Ada is in Fishers Landing with a friend for the day. If you'll excuse me, I need to check on the dinner."

Dee followed her but motioned for Julia to stay. "I'll help Emma. We womenfolk need to catch up."

While she pulled the baked fish out of the oven and Dee put the mashed potatoes, green beans, and candied carrots on the table, Emma asked her about the connection between Julia and William. Dee shrugged, but a twinkle in her eye verified the two were indeed interested in one another. How providential!

Before long, Emma called her company to dinner, and as they stood around the dining room table, William scanned the full table of food and rubbed his belly. "This looks scrumptious. Thank you for having us."

Emma motioned for them to sit. "I'm glad you all could join us."

As they settled around the table, Dee glanced around their cozy cottage. "You've made quite a home for yourself, Emma. It's charming."

"Thank you. Living on Rock Island has its challenges, but the river is so peaceful." She loved her island home, but would there truly be peace as a family one day?

The dinner conversation unfolded as a delightful exchange of lighthearted banter, filled with laughter and cheer. As the meal concluded, Michael led the men toward the lighthouse for an exploration of its fascinating secrets.

Dee and Julia stayed to help her clean up the remnants of the feast. When Dee excused herself to visit the privy, Julia asked questions while she dried the dishes Emma had washed. "You lived in Brockville most of your life, but then you moved to Thousand Island Park, right? Now you're here on Rock Island. Those were big changes. However do you endure the isolation here after being at the Park?"

Emma handed her a bowl to wipe dry while answering. "I've found that living on an island means facing challenges head on. There will be storms, both in the weather and in your heart. But there's also blessing in it—the way the Thousand Islands community comes together, the special moments of happiness, and the quiet serenity when the waves lull you to sleep. I'm learning to find peace in it."

Julia nodded, absorbing her words. "And what about love? How does that work with a lightkeeper's hours?"

Was her niece thinking of marrying William? Her gaze drifted out the window. "Love on an island is like the ebb and flow of the tide. It requires patience, understanding, and a willingness to weather the storms together, especially when your husband has an eleven-year-old daughter. But when you share a love for each other, the island, and its rhythms, and you trust the good Lord to be with you in your journey, it's a bond that can withstand anything."

Julia faltered before asking another question. "Is it difficult, taking on the role of a stepmother?"

She took a deep breath before answering. Then a sigh escaped her lips, carrying with it a weight of experience and contemplation. "At times, yes. Stepping into the role as mother poses its own set of challenges, but woven within those challenges lies a profound calling. Ada needs me—needs us, together."

The intricate dance between difficulty and reward inherent in the journey of marriage and parenting had its own benefits. Obstacles might litter the path ahead, yet commitment and unity for the sake of the family they were building together mattered most.

For a long while, Emma and her niece discussed what was in Julia's heart—especially about marriage—and Emma tried to provide her with wise counsel. She prayed that, one day, she could do the same with Ada.

Would that ever be possible?

Once the Dodges and Julia left, Michael prepared to fetch Ada from Fishers Landing. "I'll be back with our girl soon, love, but I have a suggestion."

Emma tilted her head. "What is it, sweetheart?"

"It's probably best to avoid any talk of Julia. Seems Ada has a jealous streak when it comes to you and your niece."

Emma's eyes sparked. "Perhaps you're right. Mum's the word."

He kissed her cheek and gave her a hug before leaving. "Thanks for understanding, dear. We'll figure this out—hopefully, sooner rather than later."

He rowed the skiff a mere quarter mile to the shore and walked the two blocks to collect his daughter. After thanking Elsa's family, he and Ada returned to the island.

But something was different. Gone was her feistiness, and she barely spoke about her day with her friend. Usually, she'd prattle on a mile a minute sharing all the details of her outings.

"What's wrong, sweetheart? Didn't you have a good time?" Michael prodded her as he helped her step out of the skiff and guided her to the cottage. She felt warm to the touch. Flushed.

"I don't feel well."

"What hurts?"

She put a hand to her throat and the other to her forehead. "My throat and head. Can I go to bed?"

He felt her forehead with the back of his hand. It was hot. "Goodness! You must have a fever. Yes, off to bed with you, sweetheart. We'll bring up some headache powders and a cold cloth."

"Thanks, Papa."

Ada shuffled into the parlor, her face flushed and eyes heavy. She didn't stop to greet Emma. Didn't even acknowledge her. She just climbed the stairs slowly.

Emma glanced toward the staircase and set her darning aside. "What's wrong with Ada?"

Michael shrugged. "I think she has a fever, and she says she has a sore throat and headache."

Emma jumped up from her chair. "I'll get the powders and a cold cloth. If her fever is high, we need to get it down."

Emma's disquietude warmed his heart. She really did care about Ada, despite his daughter's prickliness toward his wife. "What can I do to help?"

"A cup of ice, perhaps. If her throat hurts, she won't want to drink, but she needs to stay hydrated."

He kissed her on the forehead. "I've got it. Thanks for caring."

She froze, confusion flashing through her silvery eyes like lightning. "I love her, Michael. I'm here for her. I'm her mother now."

He wrapped her in his arms and held her tightly. "Thank you, Emma. I love you."

This time, she kissed him. "Skedaddle, darling. Meet me upstairs."

Once he'd chipped a cupful of ice pieces, he hurried upstairs to Ada's room to find his girl arguing with Emma. "I can't swallow. It hurts."

Emma smoothed her forehead with a wet rag. "But this medicine will help you feel better. I know it's hard, but if you'll swallow it, you'll be glad you did."

Michael intervened. "Come on, honey. You've got to take the medicine. I have some ice chips that will help too."

Instead of arguing, Ada pasted her lips together and squeezed her eyes shut. His girl could be a stubborn thing.

"Okay, then. I'll just go get the doctor, and he may force you to take the medicine."

Her eyes grew big, and slowly, she sat up and drank the medicine.

But as she drank, Emma looked at him with a worried frown. She turned back to Ada. "Honey, may I look at your chest? It looks as though you have a rash. Poison ivy, maybe?"

Ada waved her off. "Not you! Papa."

He shook his head. "Emma is much better at

such things, Ada. Besides, you're becoming a young woman, and it's best to let another lady help."

Ada acquiesced. Emma checked her and whispered, "Her chest and back have a crimson rash that has crept up her neck."

Ada laid down and squirmed. "It's itchy."

His worry deepened, and he felt her forehead again. Should he go for the doctor tonight? The sun was setting, and he needed to be at his post.

He pressed his palm against her cheek. Too warm. "I'm sorry you're feeling poorly, sweetheart. Hopefully, the medicine will do the trick, and you'll be right as rain by morning." He propped the pillow under her head and tucked the blanket around her.

Emma took his hand. "I'll take good care of her, Michael. You needn't worry."

Ada moaned. "I don't want you! I want Papa!"

Alarm flashed in Emma's eyes, and she whispered, "May I see you outside for a moment?" She followed him into the hallway. "It might be scarlet fever, Michael. You should get the doctor."

Michael gasped. "Scarlet fever can be fatal."

Emma grasped his hands and held them tight. She gazed into his eyes with such compassion and love that he calmed down. "Not always. My sisters had it when they were small. I helped take care of them. Both are fine. But Ada was around others at Fishers Landing, and the doctor will want to post a quarantine."

"I'll light the lamp first and make sure it'll stay lit for several hours. No telling where I'll find the doctor on a Sunday night. Please take care of her."

"I will. You can count on it. Now go, and hurry back." Emma hugged him.

Thankfully, he returned within the hour, grateful Dr. Patterson had followed him in his own skiff so Michael could tend to the light. The thought of Ada being sick made his stomach churn, and after a thorough examination, the physician verified what Emma had thought. Ada had scarlet fever.

The doctor spoke to them in the hallway, away from Ada. "It's early yet. The rash will spread to her face and other parts of her body. She may feel nauseous too. She's got a strawberry tongue, so it's moving rather fast, I suspect."

Michael frowned. "What's that?"

"Her tongue is red and swollen with little bumps. The white coating may peel off later on, so don't be surprised."

Emma was calm and confident. "Myrtle had that. It made her tongue bright red and tender for weeks."

Dr. Patterson pointed to Emma. "You've got a gem here, Michael. Ada will be in good hands with her. I'll come back tomorrow and check on her, but for now, I need to get to the Hartford home. If Ada was playing with Elsa and others today, they all need to be quarantined."

Emma nodded. "Us too. And doctor, please send a telegram to Mr. Wiseman at Thousand Island Park. I know the community there will pray for her. Oh, and to Sister Island, please. They were here today, and though they didn't see Ada, perhaps they could catch it if Ada had already contaminated the house."

The doctor shook his head. "Doubtful. It's usually from being near the patient. But I'll telegram, anyway. Take good care of her, and I'll see you tomorrow."

Michael saw him off and checked on the light. Thank heavens it was a clear, still night. He could manage his time between the light and his sick daughter.

When he returned to Ada's room, Emma and Ada were both asleep, so he stood in the doorway, his heart heavy with anguish as he watched Ada sleeping fitfully. Her delicate features were marred with pain and her lips dry and cracked. Emma slept, too, but she held Ada's hand, her head resting on the bed while she sat on the chair next to it.

He wouldn't disturb them. He'd just watch. And pray.

He'd not been a praying man for these four years. Yes, he attended church now and then, but he'd grown distant from his faith. His once unyielding belief in God had wavered, crushed by the devastating loss he'd endured. He'd felt abandoned, left to navigate the challenges of raising his young daughter alone, and He hadn't cared for God since.

But now, faced with the sight of his child's suffering, Michael was desperate. In this moment of vulnerability, he found himself wanting to reach out to the One whom he'd all but forsaken.

As he stood there, his thoughts formed into a prayer. "Please God," he whispered, his voice trembling. "I beg you to save Ada. I know I have strayed, but we need you more than ever. Please heal her and give me strength to face whatever lies ahead."

The room remained quiet, save the soft breathing of Ada and Emma. He closed his eyes and poured out his heart, surrendering his fears and doubts and anger to God. And he forgave the God who held his deceased wife in the palm of His hand.

In that moment, peace washed over him, and a flicker of faith sparked to life. Now, Michael needed to trust that God would bring her through.

But could He bring them all through and create a happy family? He prayed for that too.

Chapter 12

Emma wasn't sure what to do with the girl. She demanded her father, but he was up in the light tower doing his job. She didn't want the ice chips, but she needed water. She refused to let Emma touch her, but she needed a sponge bath to keep her temperature down.

"Ada, sweetheart, your father is working. You need to let me help you."

The girl whimpered like a toddler. "I want my real mother and father. Not you. You hate me."

Emma sighed. No matter what she said or did, Ada had an opinion of her that was far from accurate. And it hurt. "That's not true, Ada. I wouldn't be here if I didn't care."

Ada put her hand to her forehead. "It hurts so bad. Please make it stop."

Emma gently moved the child's hand and put a cold cloth on her forehead. "That should help a little. Please try and relax. That will help too."

The child stared at her for several moments. Then her eyes darted to and fro, as if she were assessing her, sizing her up, deciding if she should trust her. Finally, she sank into the pillow and closed her eyes, but her brow still furrowed in pain.

Emma watched over her closely, her heart aching

with empathy and unease. Gaining the girl's trust was crucial in order to provide the care she needed, even though every rejection from her stung deeply.

While Ada momentarily lay still, Emma moved quietly around the room, gathering the supplies for a sponge bath and making sure everything was within reach. As she approached her, she spoke soothingly. "I know it's hard right now, but I promise I won't hurt you. I only want to help. Let's make you feel a little better, okay? And when your father comes, he'll be happy to see you improving."

Ada's eyes flickered open, uncertainty still obvious in her gaze. She hesitated for a moment, likely torn between her desire for comfort and her lingering distrust. Finally, she nodded, allowing her to help.

With gentle hands, Emma began to sponge Ada's fevered body. She worked slowly, ensuring each stroke was tender and soothing. By now, the rash had a rough, sandpaper-like texture and was likely very irritating. As the cool water touched Ada's skin, she visibly relaxed, settling deep into the pillow.

During her ministrations, Emma kept her voice low and tender. "You're doing great, Ada. Try to take deep breaths, and let the water cool you down. I'm here to help you feel better. I care about you, sweetheart, even if you don't think so sometimes."

Ada's brow softened slightly, as if Emma's

words were slowly breaking through the wall she'd built. The child's eyes, once filled with vitriol, now held a touch of vulnerability.

Emma pressed into the chance to connect with her more deeply. "You know, Ada, I may not be your birth mother, but I love you like my own. Though I'll never replace your mother, I want to add to her love. I'm here because I want to be, and I want to take care of you. We're family."

The child scrutinized her until Emma felt self-conscious, as though she had chocolate on her cheek or something. But then, Ada grabbed Emma's hand and held it tightly. Her eyes filled with tears, and her bottom lip quivered. "I'm scared."

Emma's heart swelled with compassion as she gently squeezed her hand. "I know, sweetheart. It's okay to be scared. But I promise you that I'll be right here and help you get through this."

Ada's brows rose as she whispered, "Where's Midnight? Is he lost?"

Emma stroked her forehead with the cool cloth. "He's staying in the guest room, sleeping soundly on the bed. Your papa thought that best since I'm allergic."

"Papa's smart. I'm going to try and sleep now. Thank you for being here, Emma." Without waiting for an answer, Ada closed her eyes and took a deep breath.

As the hours passed, Emma remained by Ada's

side. She resolved to weather the storm and love Ada through it, and it gave her strength for the task ahead.

Michael came to check on them several times throughout the night, but Ada never woke. "Thank you for being with her, Emma. She's never been sick before, save a summer cold now and then. And I admit, I'm not a very good nursemaid. After Mary's terrible illness, well . . ."

Emma touched his arm gently. "I'm glad to help. I helped my mother care for my sisters, who tended to be sickly little things, including the bout with scarlet fever. I consider it a privilege to love and serve."

He kissed her passionately. "You're a treasure, Emma. Thank you. I'd better get back to the light. It's been finicky lately, and I wouldn't want it to go out."

"You go do your job. I'll do mine. She's safe in my care."

When he left, she adjusted the pillows, ensuring that Ada was in a comfortable position. Then she dimmed the lantern to create a peaceful atmosphere for what she hoped would be restful sleep. By the light of the moon, she continued to soothe her patient with cool cloths.

And she prayed. Prayed God would be merciful. Prayed Ada's fever would break, and she'd have no lasting consequences from the sickness.

Scarlet fever. Such a terrible disease. She

feared the worst was yet to come. Her sister had a terrible ear infection that caused her to be deaf in one ear. The neighbor's child went blind. A schoolmate died.

Emma struggled to tamp down her worries and returned to prayer. As the night wore on, her prayers became a steady practice in between cooling Ada's brow with a cold cloth and checking her blossoming rash. And though she feared for the girl, she held Ada's hand several times as she prayed, feeling the warmth of her fevered skin as she offered words of comfort and hope to the unconscious child.

Hours stretched on in eerie silence, and clouds hid the moonlight. Only Ada's shallow breathing and an occasional moan pierced the darkness. Emma's care could provide comfort and strength to the child even if her presence alone couldn't heal her.

Near daybreak, when Michael came into the room, he held a large pitcher of ice chunks. Emma took it and set it on the table as Ada stirred, her brow damp with perspiration. A faint whisper escaped her lips. "Papa."

He hurried to her side and kissed her fevered forehead, brushing back her wet hair. His eyes flashed fear, but he pasted on a quivering smile just the same. "My little darlin', you're a brave warrior. Keep on fighting this, and we'll go fishing all day long once you're well. You can even stay up late into the night and watch the stars with me too. Just you mind that."

"Stay with me, Papa. It hurts." Ada grabbed his hand, and two fat tears rolled down her cheeks.

He glanced at Emma, his face contorted with fear and sadness. He turned back to Ada and frowned. "Oh darlin', there's a thick fog bank rolling in, so I have to stay at my post and keep the boaters safe. I must keep the lamp lit and watch out for danger. But Emma is here, and believe me, she's a better nurse than I could ever be. Trust her, sweetheart. She loves you."

Ada's eyes fluttered open, and she looked at her father and then at Emma. A moment later, she closed her eyes again. Emma felt her head and tugged Michael toward the hallway.

Michael groaned. "The rash is spreading, and her cheeks are so flushed." His voice cracked with emotion.

"I'm afraid it's going to get worse before she gets better. But don't worry. I've dealt with this before. You go back to your post and keep folks safe. I'll keep our girl safe, too, God willing."

Michael rubbed his ear. "The doctor may not be able to come in this fog."

She waved off his concerns. "There's not much he can do but tell me what I'm already doing. Pray for her, Michael, will you?"

"Of course. I've been praying all night, and I'll not stop until she's up and well."

"Me either. Now go, my love." She gave him a hug, and he kissed the top of her head, a tradition that was becoming one of her favorites.

When she returned to Ada, her breathing was alarmingly shallow. Emma gave her another sponge bath with a cloth she'd dipped in icy cold water, hoping Ada would draw in a deep breath and breathe more deeply.

She did, but surprisingly, she didn't complain about the cold. That worried Emma even more.

Emma patted Ada's cheeks and forehead with the cool cloth until the child's eyes fluttered open. "Can you take some more medicine? It'll help you sleep."

Ada didn't say anything. She just looked at her. So vulnerable. So helpless. So weak.

So loved. She really did love the child. She recalled the intelligent conversations they had enjoyed together and the moments of laughter when Ada shared a joke or riddle. Despite her sass and stubbornness, Emma loved her deeper and stronger than she ever thought she could.

But what if she didn't make it through this? What if Ada died under her watch? Would Michael ever forgive her? Would she forgive herself?

Her heart quaked at the thought. No! She wouldn't let that happened. She couldn't.

She pushed away the fear that began to choke her and gave it to God.

But what if God had other plans?

• • •

The next night, Michael returned to the lighthouse, the weight of his daughter's illness pressing in on him. She was worse than before. Just moments ago, Emma had come rushing to him as he prepared to go up to work, her eyes wide with panic.

"Michael, she's running a high fever, and I can't get it to come down. We need the doctor."

Michael had shoved down his own panic. He'd smoothed her sleeve along the length of her arm. "The fog is rolling in heavier than ever. Let me check the light, then I'll decide what to do."

His chest tight with the weight of his responsibilities, he climbed the spiral staircase to the lamp room where the wick was barely flickering. Why was this fool thing being so touchy? He'd installed a new wick, filled the oil reserve.

He had to keep it shining brightly through this fog, which was growing thicker by the minute. He grabbed his tools and adjusted several mechanisms, and to his relief, the flame grew higher and higher until he had to turn it down a little.

Crisis averted. At least this one.

As he scanned the dense fog through the windows, his nerves prickled to attention. How would he see a ship in danger? If he left his post, would a ship tragedy add to his failures that seemed to pile higher and higher? He prided himself on his unwavering dedication to his role as lighthouse keeper. And yet, putting his job first had harmed his family.

Michael stepped onto the damp parapet and drew in a sharp breath. A ship's mast was barely visible through the swirling mist. The idea of leaving the ship to crash against the rocky shoal was unthinkable, and yet so was turning his back on his daughter in her hour of greatest need.

Scarlet fever. He'd known several to die from the disease. Please, God, not Ada.

"Lord, what am I to do? My child needs me, but how can I abandon that ship?"

The words caught in his throat, the familiar sting of guilt and uncertainty welling up within him. His heart ached, torn between two equally pressing obligations.

Closing his eyes, Michael took a steadying breath and offered up a silent prayer. *Lord, I've always relied on my own strength, my own judgment, to guide me through these trials. But it's not working.* He paused, his grip tightening around the railing as he opened his eyes and gazed out at the foggy night. *Show me the way, Lord, for I cannot bear the thought of failing either my duty or my child.*

A strange sense of peace washed over him, a quiet conviction that he was no longer alone in this struggle. With a renewed sense of purpose, he hurried from the tower and down to the rocky shore, his trusted porch lantern in hand. The ship was drifting dangerously close to the treacherous shoals nearby.

As he waved the lantern back and forth, signaling the ship's crew, a flicker of movement caught his eye. A small boat making its way toward the shore! As Michael squinted against the darkness, a lone figure rowed toward him with determined strokes.

As the boat drew closer, a sailor with a weathered visage called out, "Ahoy, there. We saw your signal. What's the trouble?"

Michael took a deep breath, his mind racing. Was this his opportunity to get help for Ada? "I was warning you of the shoals just there." He pointed, still holding the lantern aloft. "But my daughter has taken ill, and we desperately need the doctor. I know it's way past midnight, but . . ."

The sailor tipped his hat. "Say no more. I'll fetch the doctor straightaway. And I'll tell my crew about the shoals on my way."

A wave of relief washed over him. "God bless you, sir. I'll be forever in your debt."

As the rowboat pivoted and headed past the ship and on toward the mainland, Michael walked along the shore, using his lantern to help guide the crew past the dangerous shoals of Rock Island. "Thank you, Lord. Thank you." He murmured the words as he went, tears easing from his eyes.

Gratitude squeezed his heart. And not just for

the way God had sent the sailor. God has also given him Emma. What if he hadn't married her when he did? At this very moment, he'd be alone with Ada and would have had no one here to help.

With a deep breath, he forced himself to focus on the task at hand. After all, Emma was caring for Ada, and the ships navigating the treacherous waters of the St. Lawrence relied on the beacon's steady light—and him.

Slowly, his vision became clear, even though the river fog remained. He couldn't change the past, nor could he predict the future, but he could do everything in his power to be a better husband and father from now on. Once the fog lifted, he would press through his propensity to be silent, to be lenient, to avoid conflict. He'd apologize and make amends as best he could. He'd find a way. Somehow.

Indeed, the fog did lift about two hours later, and the doctor came, and Michael left the light to take the doctor to his daughter. They quietly climbed the cottage steps to find Emma tending to Ada's needs with unwavering devotion. He took a moment to watch them from the doorway, though neither she nor Ada seemed to notice.

Emma patiently held a glass of water as Ada took a shaky sip. Then his wife dipped the cloth into a pan of water and cooled Ada's skin with it.

Dr. Patterson leaned over and whispered, "You've got a prize there, Michael."

He nodded, but when they drew near the bed, his heart bottomed out. Ada's eyes were sunken, her face flushed, and the rash seemed to cover every inch of her. He planted a kiss on her brow. Indeed, as Emma had said, her fever seemed higher than ever.

And Ada barely responded. Only her eyes pleaded with him to help. Her lashes fluttered shut and her brow furrowed.

Emma nodded to the doctor. "Thank you for coming. What can we do?"

The doctor felt Ada's forehead. "Get some ice."

"Yes, sir, and I'll make her some herbal tea. It might soothe her throat."

Michael squeezed her hand as she brushed past him. "We'll watch over her. Thanks, Emma, for all you're doing."

Emma glanced at Ada with such affection, it drew a lump to his throat. "My pleasure."

As the doctor examined Ada, Michael sat beside her sickbed. His daughter was as still as a corpse, and his heart swelled with love, anxiety—and fear. He gently brushed his fingers against her forehead, tracing the rough bumps of the rash that marred her delicate skin.

"I love you, Ada." His voice cracked from the tenderness he felt. "I've been praying for you, trusting God for your recovery."

To his surprise, Ada's eyes fluttered open. "Prayed?" She spoke in a whisper. "You haven't prayed since Mama . . ."

His breath caught in his throat, and he took a moment to gather his thoughts. Dr. Patterson glanced at him but continued taking Ada's pulse with his finger on her wrist.

Michael's own pain and grief had caused him to distance himself from his faith, leaving a void where prayer once resided. But in that moment, faced with his daughter's illness, he had to confront his neglect.

"You're right, Ada. I have neglected my relationship with our Savior for far too long. But that stops now. We need His guidance and strength, especially during this difficult time."

A faint smile played on Ada's lips. "Emma prays," she whispered. "All the time. She prays for me and you."

"How are you feeling, Ada?" Dr. Patterson interrupted them.

Ada mustered the strength to free her arms from the confines of the covers and weakly rubbed her stomach. "My tummy hurts." Visibly depleted from the effort, she allowed her arms to fall back to her sides.

Dr. Patterson released her wrist with a slight frown. "That's normal, Ada. But remember, even when it's hard, try to drink. It will help you heal and regain your strength. You're in safe hands with Emma, young lady. She knows just what to do."

After the physician left, having given further instructions for Ada's care, Emma returned to the room, carefully balancing a heavy tray with three cups, a pitcher of ice chips, a steaming pot of tea, and two bowls of stew. It was a small gesture, but it spoke volumes of Emma's dedication.

Michael gratefully took the tray from her and set it on the table, his eyes meeting her sweet smile. Despite her having been up all night caring for Ada, she remained strong and positive.

She handed him a bowl. "The stew is for us. The tea is for our girl."

He nodded and took a big bite. He hadn't realized how hungry he was. And tired. It was nearly five o'clock, and the stress of Ada's illness, maintaining the light, and guiding the endangered ship through the fog had sapped his strength.

Glancing at Emma, he felt a pang of guilt. She must be just as tired.

"Thank you for taking care of Ada. Would you like to rest for a while?"

Emma sank down onto a nearby chair, her weariness evident. "After I eat, I'd like to freshen up a bit, if that's okay."

"I'll keep an eye on the light through that window, and when you're done, you can rest here as well. How about I make a pallet for us to use when we're tending her? It might be a few days until she recovers." His voice reflected his newfound determination.

Emma's eyes flashed worry, and she bit her lip. Perhaps he was a little too cavalier in his assessment of how quickly Ada would recover? But she rose to do as he encouraged her to.

He followed her to the doorway and whispered, "Is she going to be all right, Emma? Did the doctor say something? You look worried."

Emma shook her head. "We still have a long journey toward recovery, but we must trust that God will get her through." Her voice trembled, just a little, and her words held a veiled warning.

Was Ada still in more danger than he realized?

Chapter 13

Three long and scary days later, Emma faithfully wiped the sweat from Ada's forehead and murmured soothing words. They had feared the worst, and the doctor did, too, but Michael and she prayed continually, both apart and together. Praying with her husband was an unexpected gift in such a dark time, and she was grateful for the moments they had together fighting for their girl through prayer.

By midmorning, she sensed a shift in Ada's condition, a subtle change that hinted at the possibility of recovery. The fever seemed less intense, and Ada's breathing became steadier.

As the day progressed, Ada's condition slowly improved. Her fever began to recede, and moments of lucidity cut through the haze of the illness. Then, for the first time in three days, Ada's eyes fluttered open, and Emma's heart swelled with joy at the sight of the child regaining consciousness after battling the ravages of scarlet fever.

She breathed a sigh of relief as she touched Ada's cheek. Her temperature felt almost normal. "Well, hello, my precious girl. It's good to see you awake again."

Ada smiled weakly, gratitude blossoming on

her face. "You . . . you stayed with me all the time?" Her whisper was hoarse but filled with appreciation.

Emma brushed back her matted hair. The rash had receded somewhat, but it still gave her a flushed and spotted complexion. "Of course, Ada. You're not alone in this, or anything. As long as I have breath in my lungs, I'll be here. Your papa has been here, too, as much as he could, and we've been praying for you day and night."

When Michael brought the doctor in to examine Ada, Dr. Patterson was encouraging. "She'll make it through, thank the Lord, and Emma, you've been a big reason for that. A trained nurse couldn't have done more."

Michael took her hand and squeezed it. "I don't know what we would have done without her, Doctor. Emma is a godsend to all of us."

The physician nodded. "That she is, and don't you forget it, Michael. By the way, the fever hasn't spread. No one in Fishers Landing has it."

Emma clapped her hands together. "Thank the good Lord."

"The Sister Island folks are fine too. They telegrammed me yesterday."

Michael grinned. "A triple blessing, I say! Thank you, Doctor, for the good news."

After Dr. Patterson had left, Emma prepared warm herbal tea to soothe Ada's still-sore throat and tongue, and Ada sipped it cautiously. By the evening, her hunger had returned, and she drank some chicken broth. She was healing, and though she remained terribly weak, she didn't seem to have any lasting complications from the disease.

As the days passed and Ada's recovery progressed, Emma did everything she could to make their confinement in the lighthouse cottage more bearable. She stayed by Ada's side, offering words of comfort and reading her favorite stories aloud, distracting her from her waning discomfort and providing a soothing presence. She gave her gentle massages to help alleviate her muscle aches, and as her rash began to fade and her tongue heal, her energy levels improved.

Every day, while Emma prepared a meal, Michael brought Midnight in to see Ada. Thankfully, Emma's thoughtful husband put a sheet over Ada's bed and removed it before she returned so she wouldn't have to deal with her allergies, though at times, she still sneezed uncontrollably.

Several nights, while Ada slept peacefully, Emma snuck up to the lamp room to visit with Michael. They cherished tender kisses and embraces, prayed together, and talked about the future when all this was passed.

On several occasions, Emma told stories of her childhood adventures to Ada. "Can I tell you a story about when I was your age?"

Ada nodded, a smile beckoning her to share. "Please. I like stories about you."

Emma settled on the edge of Ada's bed, gently brushing a stray lock of hair from her flushed face. "When I was about your age, I had a rather . . . embarrassing experience that has stayed with me to this day."

Ada's eyebrows raised, and she reached out to grasp her hand. "What happened?"

She gave the child's hand a gentle squeeze before continuing. "Well, I was playing in the old oak tree at the edge of our property. I loved that tree, and I would spend hours climbing up and down its sturdy branches." A faint smile tugged at the corners of her lips, but it quickly faded as the memory resurfaced. "One day, I climbed a little too high, and I got stuck. I couldn't figure out how to get back down, and I was starting to panic."

Ada's eyes widened. "That must have been scary."

Emma nodded. "It was. But what made it even worse was that some of my schoolmates walked by and saw me up there. Instead of trying to help, they just laughed at me." A shudder ran through her, and she closed her eyes, the humiliation of that moment still pricking at her. "They thought it was so funny, seeing me stuck and afraid. They just kept laughing and mocking me."

Ada squeezed Emma's hand even tighter. "That was mean."

Emma opened her eyes, a sad smile on her lips.

"Sometimes, when people are unkind, they don't realize the power that their words and actions can have or how deeply their laughter or mockery can hurt someone." She paused, her gaze meeting Ada's. "Your papa said you've experienced something similar with girls at school who've been cruel to you."

A single tear trailed down her cheek. "They . . . they make fun of me, just like those children did to you. And it hurts so much."

Emma reached up, gently wiping the tear away with her thumb. "I know how that feels. But you must remember that their words and actions say far more about them than they do about you."

Ada's lips quivered. "I've said some mean things to you too. I'm sorry, Emma."

Emma's heart clenched. "Oh, sweet girl, I forgive you. But always remember the power of words and actions, and how they can lift others up or tear them down." She pressed a tender kiss to Ada's forehead. "From now on, let's vow to be kind to others. Does that sound like a good plan?"

Ada furrowed her brow. "Even when friends make fun of you? Two girls at school use my name wrong. They laugh at me and say, 'Die, you bean polder.' It's 'cuz I'm skinny and my name is Diepolder."

Emma huffed, placing her hands on her hips. "That's not funny. That is mean. I'm sorry, sweetheart. Jesus said that if you even wish someone ill, you're committing murder in your heart. That's a sin. How about we pray for them, Ada?"

They did, and in the process, Emma guided Ada to forgive the girls. When they finished praying, Ada smiled. "I feel better. Thanks, Emma."

Over the next few days, meaningful conversations became more frequent, and Emma's heart soared at her growing camaraderie and kinship with Ada. Michael lent a hand whenever he could, but his duties kept him busy a lot of the time.

As Ada's strength gradually returned, she and the girl played card games, and she taught Ada to play cat's cradle. She tied a loop of string and showed her how to work through the figures.

"Cat's cradle is a string game involving creating various figures with a loop of string maneuvered through the hands. Versions can be played by either one or two people, sometimes more. Each figure created has a different name, but I don't remember what they are called."

Emma wound the string around her fingers and guided Ada how to take it from her and make a new shape. Then Emma continued the process. Ada loved the game, and throughout her convalescence, she begged to play it over and over again.

They were slowly but surely forming a bond, and Emma rejoiced at the progress they were making.

One morning, Michael brought them each a bouquet of wildflowers. "Good morning, ladies! I thought you could use a bit of cheering up. Picked them myself."

Ada took the flowers and smelled them. "Thanks, Papa. They're beautiful."

Emma agreed. "That was very thoughtful, Michael. Thank you."

Suddenly, Ada thrust the flowers toward Emma. "I want you to have these, Emma. As a thank you for all you've done. Do you mind, Papa? It's all I can give her right now."

Michael's eyes misted, and he smiled wide. "How thoughtful, darling. Of course, I don't mind."

Emma swallowed the lump in her throat as she gratefully took the flowers. "Thank you, Ada. How about we share them? They can brighten the room as we enjoy our time together."

Ada's smile lit up, and Emma felt like dancing. But a little piece of her wondered if this peaceful harmony would last.

Michael stood at the edge of the bed, his heart heavy with conflicting emotions. Ada and Emma laughed together, their bond strengthened by Emma's unwavering care during Ada's illness. The sight should have filled him with joy, but instead, confusion gnawed at him.

He had grieved over Ada's hostility toward

Emma and pondered how to help change her. He had hoped that time would improve things, that he could be a binding force between Ada and Emma. But it seemed his daughter's transformation had been brought about, not by his efforts, but by Emma's ceaseless care for her while she was sick.

Would he be left out of their circle as Emma had been?

When Emma received the flowers he had picked for Ada, a tiny twinge of shame engulfed him. The gesture was meant to be a peace offering. Instead, it reinforced the divide he felt growing between himself and his girls, reminding him of his failures as the head of his home as a father and husband.

Ada broke into his thoughts. "Let's play cat's cradle, Emma."

Neither Ada nor Emma seemed to even notice he was there. Emma handed her a string. "You start this time. Let's see how many moves we can make before we get tangled up." She looked up and beckoned him to join them. "Michael, come and see how adept your daughter is at cat's cradle. My sisters were never this good."

He did, but found little joy in it. The alienation he felt was his own fault. He should've been more proactive, should have stepped in to help with Ada's recovery more. Moreover, he'd had duties to fulfill as the lightkeeper, responsibilities that pressed on him day and night.

He chastised himself. "Excuses. Excuses."

Emma's fingers paused in midair, the string displaying an intricate design. "Sorry, Michael. What did you say?"

He shook his head. "Nothing, sweetheart. Keep playing your game."

Emma held out the string, and Ada took it, forming another intricate figure. He'd neglected his new bride, too, expecting her to take the lion's share of caring for his Ada.

Just then, the girls burst into peals of laughter. Ada turned to him. "We made thirteen figures this time. The most ever!"

Michael pasted on a smile. "That's nice, honey, but I'd better get back to work." At least there he felt he was needed.

Ada and Emma both waved, but they had already returned to another round of their game.

Taking a deep breath, he went to the kitchen, poured a cup of coffee, and sat at the table. He scolded himself. "Why should I wallow in my failures? I love my wife and daughter. I want to be all they need me to be. Help me, God, please."

He couldn't let regret or jealousy consume him. He had to forgive himself, step up, and be the father Ada needed and the husband Emma desired, even if it meant acknowledging his past mistakes and changing his ways.

With another gulp of his coffee, he mustered the courage to talk to them. But first, he grabbed a puzzle box from the parlor wardrobe and dusted it off. He'd put it together last winter, when he was alone, and now, perhaps the three of them could put it together. Maybe that could be a start.

When he entered Ada's room, his girls looked up from the picture they were drawing together. Emma tilted her head. "Is everything okay? I thought you were going to work in the shop."

"Emma. Ada." His voice cracked with emotion. "I want to apologize to you. I've let my own fears and insecurities keep me distant. Truth is, sickness scares me, especially when it reminded me of your mama's illness, Ada. I've stayed away far too much, and I'm truly sorry. I left you to do most of the work, Emma, and I've neglected you, my sweet daughter, when you needed me the most."

Ada blinked, her confusion evident on her raised brow. "Oh, Papa. It's okay. I was sleeping most of the time, and Emma helped when I wasn't. Don't worry. You're a good papa, and I'm getting better every day."

Emma rushed over to him and planted a tender kiss on his whiskery cheek. Her face lit up with love. "Michael, I wouldn't have traded these past days for anything. It gave me the chance to get to know this little lady. I think providence had a hand in all of it. Besides, you're a wonderful father, just you mind that."

Ada, summoning her strength, climbed out of

bed and hugged him. It was a weak hug but a heartfelt one. Michael's heart soared, and he swallowed the rock that had formed in his throat, clearing it.

"Want to do a puzzle together?" He held up the box with a picture of a tranquil forest scene on it.

Emma and Ada nodded, but their excitement waned when they glanced around the room. Ada frowned. "We don't have a puzzle table."

Michael chuckled. "I'll bring the side table up from the parlor and grab the chair from the guest room."

Emma rubbed her hands together. "I'll make some tea and bring up some sandwiches. Let's have a party. The three of us."

Ada giggled. "Yes. Let's celebrate me getting better."

Before long, the three of them gathered around the makeshift puzzle table, their collective efforts warming Michael's heart. As they worked, the weight of his past mistakes began to lift, replaced by a sense of hope. It wasn't too late to be the father and husband he should be. He would fit the pieces of his family back together, piece by piece.

As they sat around the table interlocking puzzle pieces, they chomped on egg salad sandwiches, sipped on tea, and worked as a team. Their conversation flowed effortlessly.

Ada slipped an edge piece into place, her eyes

revealing delight. "Papa, tell me about Mama. I can hardly remember her anymore."

Michael glanced at Emma, her gentle smile encouraging him to share. "Your mama was a remarkable woman, Ada. She had a gentle spirit and loved to paint. She always saw the beauty in the world, even during the toughest times."

Emma chimed in, her voice filled with admiration. "I've seen some of her paintings, and they are beautiful. You inherited her artistic talent, you know."

Ada grinned, a hint of pride in her eyes. "Really? I wish I could see them."

He nodded. "I have some of them stored away in my workshop. When you're feeling better, I'll show them to you. Your mama would be so proud of you, Ada."

Their conversation continued as they worked on the puzzle, sharing stories, memories, and dreams. They talked about their favorite books and places they'd like to visit someday. They laughed at silly jokes and playfully teased each other, the jesting finally free of Ada's cutting sarcasm.

When they talked about their fears, Emma turned to Michael. "I understand that sickness is scary, especially after what you've been through. But you never have to face anything alone. We are here for you, Ada and I, and we'll support each other through the good times and the bad. Right, Ada?"

Ada smiled. "Right! We're the three musketeers!"

At that, the three of them laughed heartily, Michael's heart full of joy. "How could I be so blessed to have two wonderful women watching over me?"

Emma chuckled. "We feel the same about you, Michael."

She winked at Ada, and Ada winked back. What had those two been talking about when he was preoccupied? Seemed as though they had secrets.

As they neared the completion of the puzzle, a sense of accomplishment and unity filled the room. Emma clicked the final piece in place, creating the beautiful forest image that reminded him of the harmony he felt.

He sat back, admiring their handiwork, and basked in the joy they shared. It wasn't just the completed puzzle. It was the connection he experienced with them.

"I'm tired." Ada reminded him of a wilting flower. She still had a way to go before she was back to her old self. He stood and scooped her into his arms, and she giggled. "I'm a little big to be carried, Papa."

He kissed her cheek. "You'll always be my baby girl. Let's get you in bed so you can rest."

She kissed him back. "And you'll always be the best papa in the whole wide world."

Michael sighed. Could life get any better?

Chapter 14

As the days turned into a week, Emma continued to care for Ada. She meticulously attended to every detail, providing her with nourishing meals and offering her emotional support when she was tired, weak, or hurting. The child's flushed complexion gradually faded, and little by little, she grew stronger.

Emma moved the small puzzle table near the window where Ada could sit and bask in the sunlight to indulge in quiet activities such as drawing or writing in her journal. She brought her books about nature and adventure, sparking Ada's imagination and helping her escape momentarily from the confines of her room.

She cherished each moment she spent with Ada, and they celebrated each milestone of her recovery. When Michael was present, they sat together in the cozy kitchen sharing meals and enjoying time together.

Slowly, Ada's appetite began to return, and her sore throat eased. Emma prepared meals with love and care, making sure they were not only nutritious but also appetizing, to entice Ada's tender taste buds.

One evening, as the three of them enjoyed a delicious meal of chicken—which Emma cut into tiny pieces for Ada—mashed potatoes, and softly cooked carrots, Ada tilted her head, a glint in her eyes. "I have a question for you both."

Emma exchanged a cheery glance with Michael, pleased the girl's childish wonder was returning. "What's your question, Ada?"

She leaned forward. "If you could do or be anything, what would it be or what would you do?"

Michael shrugged. "That's easy. I'd go down to Rochester and move your school here, right onto this island, so that you could go to classes and yet I could see you every day. I hate it when you're away, and I am not looking forward to you leaving us."

Ada rolled her eyes. "Oh, Papa."

Emma knew the child was looking for something more lighthearted. "I agree with your father, but me? I'd love to fly like an angel. Imagine soaring through the sky and diving into the clouds. Oh, how I'd love to feel the wind in my hair and fly up and down the St. Lawrence River and count the islands and wave hello to everyone I see. But most of all, I'd love to look down at the world and see life from God's perspective! Wouldn't that be grand?"

"I saw an angel. He was beautiful—and nice too." Ada's comment held a resoluteness that made Emma sit up straight.

Michael's brows furrowed, and his face blanched. "You saw an angel? When, my darling?"

"When I was sick. I heard you and Emma

praying near my bed, but my eyelids were too heavy to open them. Then I saw the angel. He was shining white, whiter than snow, and he told me to trust God, that I would get strong and be better. His voice was calm and soothing, and it made me happy. After that, I didn't worry anymore. I just slept for a really long time."

Emma gasped. So did Michael. She touched the girl's thin arm. "Oh, Ada. You've been given a special gift from God. Not many people get to see an angel."

"I know, and God loves me. A lot. And I like talking about Him." Ada took a bite of her buttered bread and chewed nonchalantly.

Michael glanced at her and frowned. "We haven't talked much about the Lord, have we? I'm so sorry."

Ada swallowed. "Nope, but Granny doesn't talk about God either. Neither did Mama. But Emma does, and it makes me feel good." She paused for a moment before taking another bite of bread. "I'm glad my tongue doesn't hurt. This tastes so good."

Michael reached over and kissed her temple. "I think you have a good idea, darling. We'll start talking about God more. I promise."

Emma marveled that the privilege of serving Ada had not only helped to heal the child physically, but it had also touched Ada's spirit and strengthened her own, reminding her of the power of compassion and selflessness. Every tear, every laugh, every tiny conversation became a gift Emma treasured, and watching the transformation in this young girl amazed her.

Emma vowed she'd not take Ada's spiritual hunger for granted. That night, she climbed up the light tower and talked with Michael about the urgency of capturing the moment, and he agreed. "Yes, let's focus our discussions on God and His word while she's still with us. She's leaving too soon, Emma, and I'm worried for her. I don't know if she's strong enough."

Emma took his hand and kissed it. "And that's why we'll have to trust God and exercise our faith."

Michael shook his head. "Easier said than done. I've let my faith wane, and it's weak and feeble."

Emma winked encouragingly. "Then we'll just have to exercise our faith muscles, won't we?"

He chuckled. "I hadn't thought of it like that. But yes, wife, let's do that together."

In the days that followed, Emma and Michael engaged Ada in conversations about God. Michael encouraged her to take the lead, for now. He listened attentively, casting her supportive and loving glances.

They gathered in the parlor or on the porch—and occasionally strolled around the tiny island—and then they delved into discussions of faith. With Scripture in hand, Emma read passages and offered words of encouragement and reassurance. The ensuing discussions often reached profound depths.

One morning, Emma opened her Bible to the Psalms. "Today, I'd like to share a passage that's always brought me comfort. It says, 'The LORD is my strength and my shield; my heart trusted in him, and I am helped; therefore, my heart greatly rejoiceth.' "

As she spoke these words, a sense of peace settled upon the room, embracing them all. Ada sighed. "That's what the angel said, and this is how I felt when he came to me. I could feel the strength in my body."

Michael cleared his throat, tears welling up in his eyes. "Faith in God can give us the courage and strength to face any challenge that comes our way. You can take that faith with you to school and into all of your life."

As their conversations continued, they grew deeper and more poignant. When they explored the mysteries of God's love and forgiveness, Ada burst into tears. "I'm sorry, Emma. I was so mean to you when you first came here. The ants. The cruel words. The disobedience. And Midnight. Please forgive me."

Emma took her in her arms and hugged her. "Oh, my sweet girl, I've already forgiven you, remember? For all of it. Now let's put that in the past, okay?"

Ada accepted the lace handkerchief Emma offered her and blew her nose. "Okay."

As she gained strength, Ada spent more and more time outdoors, taking short walks around the tiny island or sitting on the porch to breathe in the fresh air and soak up the healing power of nature.

"I'll miss the sound of the waves crashing against the shore," Ada admitted as they strolled around the island. "And I'll miss the river."

Michael took one of her hands and Emma took the other, but he stopped and gazed at his daughter. "I need to ask you something, Ada. Do you feel like you'll be strong enough to start school in a few weeks, or should we contact the school and tell them you'll be late in coming?"

Ada looked at the ground for several moments before answering. "I'm not sure, Papa. I want to go, but let's wait and see, okay?"

Michael nodded, a worried frown crossing his lips. "Okay. We'll decide next week."

When they returned to the porch, he lit the lantern, said goodnight, and headed to the tower to light the lighthouse lamp.

Emma covered Ada with a blanket and fetched her a glass of cold milk. After she tucked the blanket around Ada's legs, she sat down to enjoy the evening. "Take a deep breath, Ada. Creation has a unique way of reminding us how to heal and grow. Sometimes we just need to sit back and take it all in."

For several long moments, they did. But then Ada broke the silence. "Can I ask you a question, Emma?"

"You can ask me anything anytime. What are you thinking?"

The child stared at her for several moments as if she wasn't sure she should ask. Finally, she seemed to find the courage. "Why do you love Papa so much?"

How should she answer that? He was a good man, but she ached to know him as a more engaged husband. She pushed away the thought and smiled. "My love for your papa goes beyond words. Your father is a good man. He's a faithful and hard worker, and he's an amazing father to you too. His heart is wide open, and he always puts others before himself. When I first met him, I saw those qualities I hold dear."

Ada listened intently, nodding at every comment. "That's why I love him too."

Emma ventured to add, "But, Ada, do you know the best gift your papa ever gave me?"

Ada shook her head, her brows furrowing.

Emma grinned. "He gave me you!"

Each time Michael had to say goodnight and retreat to the light tower, a growing sense of frustration consumed him. He no longer looked forward to the time of quiet. Instead, he despised the separation from Emma and Ada more with each passing night. Ada would be off to school soon, and he yearned to spend every precious moment with her.

As he climbed the winding stairs to the lantern room, he fretted about the days to come. Ada was getting better by the day, but would her strength be sufficient to get her through the demanding days of school once the term started? She was still so skinny and frail that it scared him.

Should he assert his fatherly authority and insist she remain with them for a while longer? Ada had begun to look forward to returning to Rochester for the start of school. She missed her friends, her granny, the bustling city life that awaited her return. She'd be heartbroken if he put his foot down and forbade her, wouldn't she?

The mere thought of being separated from Ada again filled him with an overwhelming sense of loss, a feeling that haunted him every time he said goodbye. And this year, his loss seemed so much worse after the harrowing experience of almost losing her to scarlet fever. What if she got sick again?

But he also looked forward to having Emma all to himself. To be alone, unhindered by prying eyes and listening ears. He wanted to enjoy a real honeymoon season, just as Emma did.

As the wind howled, warning him of another impending storm, Emma joined him in the light room as she'd come to do most nights once Ada was sound asleep.

Emma would be the only bright spot in Ada's departure.

While they stood on the parapet watching the clouds roll in, Emma leaned against the railing, a somber expression on her face. Her unease was palpable. Did she want to keep Ada here a little longer too?

He touched her shoulder softly. "Be right back. Seems the light isn't as bright as it should be."

He left her on the parapet and meticulously checked the light, adjusting the wick to make sure everything worked properly. When he rejoined her, her eyes looked sad. But a hint of frustration overshadowed the sorrow.

"Michael." Her voice was tinged with exhaustion. "Lately, it feels as though you're drifting apart from Ada and me amidst all the responsibilities."

Now that was not at all what he had expected.

He glanced at the revolving light. "Emma, you know how important my work is." Irritation crept up his spine and into his words. "The safety of those on the river depends on the light. I wish I could give you the undivided attention you deserve, but the lighthouse requires constant vigilance."

She nodded, but did she agree?

He loved that she had made it a daily tradition

to visit him after Ada went to sleep, but tonight he found no joy in it. Instead, he felt as though he had failed yet again.

"I need to check the lamp. The fool thing has been unreliable all evening." His tone was flat. Cold. Like he felt.

While he tinkered with the mechanisms, he couldn't help but wonder if he could ever make either Emma or Ada happy. Michael called to his wife from the light room. "I'll be right back. I need to fetch some more fuel."

"Take your time. I'm enjoying the view."

He descended the tower and grabbed the needed kerosene, warring with his thoughts. Though he often had to shove the desire aside, he yearned for more moments of solitude with Emma too. Ada's illness had eroded the precious little time alone they had enjoyed, and he, too, longed for a connection that was uninterrupted and intimate. Uninterrupted even by the light.

When he returned to the lamp room and replenished the fuel, he took Emma's hand and kissed it. "You're right, wife. I'm frustrated too. But I'm torn between wanting to be alone with you and worrying that Ada isn't well enough to leave."

Emma squeezed his hand. "I know you've worried about Ada. What's bothering you?"

He sighed, his heart full of apprehension. "I know we're both looking forward to being alone, but I can't shake this fear that she's not yet strong enough to return to school so soon after her illness. She still gets so weak and tired after just a short walk around this little island. What if something happened to her? What if she has a relapse and we're not there?"

Emma's eyes softened with empathy. "You're such a loving father, Michael, and I understand your fears. We've been through so much with her this summer, it's only natural to worry. But we have to trust in God's plan for her. He's brought her this far, helping her through every step of her recovery, and He'll lead her on."

Michael leaned forward and tugged on his earlobe. "I know, Emma, but it's so hard to let go. I'm her father, and I want to protect her from any harm. Sending her to Rochester has never been easy for me, and now, after this terrible illness, it's even harder. What if I make a mistake by allowing her to go back to school so soon?"

Emma lifted her chin, a small smile gracing her face. "Our faith in God means trusting Him with our precious girl. We've seen His faithfulness, even witnessed the miracle of her recovery. Now, we must lean on Him, surrendering our fears and anxieties to His loving care."

His eyes began to well up with tears, fear and hope warring within him. "I've never been good at relinquishing control, Emma. It's so hard. I don't know what to do."

Emma wrapped an arm around him and pulled

him close. "I love you so much for the depth of love you have for your daughter. How deeply you care. It's never easy to let go, especially when our hearts have been tested. But our love for Ada is just a tiny reflection of God's love for us. We want the best for her. God does, too, but so much more."

Michael kissed her softly. "I appreciate your faith, and your patience, Emma. My love for you is just as strong, you know."

Emma glanced at his face as if searching the depths of his heart. She nodded. "Our love is worth fighting for, even in the face of frustration and uncertainty. I love you, Michael."

He tugged her into a warm embrace as the rain began to patter on the windowpanes. They huddled together, their gentle breath mingling with the gentle sound of raindrops. As long as it remained a light rain, she would stay with him.

She hugged his arm, placing her head against it. "I'll miss Ada, too, but I can't help but dream of our future together. Whether next week or months from now, I envision romantic dinners and outings, just the two of us, where we can savor each other's company without any distractions."

He chuckled, releasing the tension he struggled with. "It sounds like a perfect life. But with your wonderful culinary talents, I might get too fat to climb the tower."

Emma giggled. "Stuff and nonsense. You're far

too busy and hardworking a man to get fat. And what about our long walks, hand in hand, along the shore?"

His pulse picked up at the thought. "And stargazing into the wee hours of the night, leisurely boat rides to visit some of our island neighbors, and fun fishing trips."

"Sounds like a dream come true, my love. And I'd like to add to that list visiting Thousand Island Park more often."

He kissed her again. "Absolutely, sweetheart. Every Sunday and more besides."

Emma sighed, and in the midst of their dreams, he sensed the unspoken question that had been lingering between them. With a gentle tone, he bridged a topic that had been quietly nestled in the recesses of his mind. "There's something I've been wondering about, something we've still yet to discuss. Do you . . . do you see children in our future?"

Emma's gaze held a mixture of surprise and curiosity. "Of course, my love, and I've been pondering that same question. Bringing a child into the world and nurturing that little life fills me with both excitement and apprehension, especially at our age."

Michael clicked his tongue. "As you say, 'stuff and nonsense,' wife. Our love and commitment will provide a strong foundation for a family, as I've seen so faithfully displayed this summer."

Emma's hand found its way to his, their fingers intertwining with quiet reassurance. "It's a thrilling thought, but I have a small concern."

"What worries you, love?"

Emma bit her bottom lip before speaking. "How will Ada feel if we have another child?"

Chapter 15

A week later, Emma entered Ada's room with a smile that grew from ear to ear. Ada was awake and full of energy as she slipped on her dress, and thankfully, Midnight was nowhere to be seen, so he wouldn't give Emma another sneezing fit.

The feisty spark that had been dimmed by scarlet fever had returned to the child's eyes, filling her with new brightness. But best of all, the illness had seemingly taken her animosity and unkindness with it. Perhaps her strawberry tongue did the work that no amount of badgering could.

Ada fumbled with her back collar button, her face scrunched up in determination.

"Good morning, sweetheart. Here, let me get those." Emma gently turned her around and buttoned her dress. "Looks like you're feeling rather chipper today."

Ada nodded, her once-whispered voice now strong and clear. "I feel great, Emma! The rash is gone, my tongue doesn't hurt, and I'm starting to feel like my old self again. I can't wait to get back to school."

"Well, young lady, I've been thinking about that. Your father and I will miss you terribly, but we know you need a good education. To celebrate your return to academic endeavors and to acknowledge you are indeed growing up fast, how about I make you a new hat, a real grownup bonnet? You see, until I took the post as librarian at Thousand Island Park, I was a skilled milliner. I worked at it for years."

With the last button closed, Ada turned to look at her, her eyes wide. "Then why do you wear that old hat?" As soon as the words came out of her mouth, she clamped both hands over her lips as if to keep any more words from coming out. She just as quickly released her hands and took a deep breath. "Sorry. That was mean."

Instead of being upset, Emma shrugged. "Thank you for the apology. That old hat is a treasured heirloom from my mother. She wore it for her wedding to my father. I know it's old and unfashionable, but somehow, it gives me comfort."

Ada frowned. "It's not so bad, really. I was just in a bad mood that day I made fun of it."

Emma waved off her concern. "It's okay, but remember to always use your words to be kind, Ada. I see you've been working hard on that, and I commend you for it. Keep up the good work, darling."

Ada nodded. "I will, Emma."

Emma took Ada's hand and tugged her to her room. "And now, let me show you my secret treasure trove of fabrics and trimmings that I have hidden in one of my steamer trunks. You can pick the fabric, lace, ribbons, and I'll make you a bonnet or a fascinator you can wear on your first day back to school."

Ada scrunched up her nose. "What's the difference?"

Emma smiled. "Well, fascinators are smaller, more decorative hats that don't have a brim or a crown, and you know what bonnets are."

"Then I definitely would like a decorative bonnet, please. Those fancy fascinators are for older girls."

Emma chuckled. One minute she wanted to be a lady and the next, to stay a little girl. "Sounds good to me, sweetheart."

Gently lifting the lid of her largest truck, Emma revealed a stunning assortment of fabrics in a rainbow of colors and textures. She showed Ada her soft silks in delicate pastels, shimmering organza, and luxurious satins. And of course, wools, cottons, linens, duck, and seersuckers for everyday wear lay at the bottom of the trunk. Ada's eyes widened with wonder as she ran her fingers over the materials.

"Such an array, Emma. How shall I ever choose?"

Emma patted her shoulder. "Well, first, what will you wear on your first day? Your uniform?"

Ada shook her head. "On the first day, we get to wear our Sunday best. After that, we have to wear our uniform, 'cept on Parents' Day and a few other special days. I'm going to wear my pink flower girl dress. Then I can tell everyone about the wedding—and you."

Emma hugged her. "You do have many tales to tell, Ada, and I'm blessed to be a part of them. But back to your new bonnet." She reached deeper into the truck and pulled out a bundle tied with a satin ribbon. She handed it to Ada. "Open it."

The girl grinned as she untied the ribbon and unwrapped the package. "It feels like Christmas!"

Inside were dainty lace appliques, intricately woven trims, and ribbons in every hue imaginable. Ada beamed, slipping her arms around Emma and hugging her tight. "This bonnet will be an heirloom for my daughter one day."

Emma's heart soared and her eyes misted. How far they'd come!

Together, Emma and Ada carefully examined the fabrics, trims, and buttons that might coordinate nicely with her dress. Ada touched the vibrant pink silk, and Emma told stories of where she had acquired the items throughout the years.

With the fabrics and trimmings carefully chosen, Emma set to work, the parlor turning into a makeshift sewing room. The sound of scissors cutting through fabric and lace filled the air as Emma meticulously crafted the perfect bonnet for Ada, her skilled hands moving with precision and care as she cut, stitched, and created.

Ada clapped her hands. "This is going to be the prettiest bonnet at school. Thanks for doing this."

"My pleasure, sweetheart. How about we add a little soft lavender lace to it to give it a bit of whimsy?"

"That's a great idea. That way, I can wear it with my lavender dress on Sundays." She picked up the lavender lace and ran her fingers over it. "It's beautiful."

Michael walked into the room and chuckled. "Has our cottage turned into a milliner shop, my dear ladies?"

Ada laughed. "No, Papa. Emma is making just one bonnet—for me!" She beamed with excitement.

Emma shrugged playfully. "Maybe two. I think it's time I make myself one too. I'm not an old maid anymore. I'm the wife of a celebrated lightkeeper and the mother of a wonderful girl."

Michael and Ada exchanged a warm glance, their smiles widening. "We love you, Emma. Don't we?" His voice was filled with affection.

Ada's eyes lit up, mirroring her father's sentiment. She didn't say the words, but her vigorous nodding conveyed her agreement. That was enough for now.

As she created, Ada stayed close by her, laughing and chatting about her friends at school, her teachers, and, of course, her beloved granny.

As the bonnet took shape, Emma listened attentively to Ada's stories, cherishing the girl's exuberance and lively spirit. Ada occasionally offered ideas, making the process feel collaborative and like a labor of love.

In the end, they agreed that a cascade of silk flowers, carefully handcrafted by Emma, would be the perfect finishing touch. That night she stayed up far past midnight completing the intricate flowers, and at long last, it was done.

At breakfast, Emma presented Ada with the finished product. Michael watched them, his smile wide and affirming. But his folded arms and raised brows hinted that he was scrutinizing it beyond the material.

Ada held her breath and squeezed her eyes shut when Emma gently placed it on her head. Soft pink silk cascaded down the side, the delicate lace framed her face perfectly, and the handmade silk flowers bloomed with soft hues. Ada looked at her reflection in the mirror, and tears ran down her cheeks.

"Don't you like it, Ada?" Emma fretted, praying she did.

"Like it? It's just the most exquisite thing I've ever seen!" She touched her hat affectionately and then hugged Emma so tight, her breath caught.

Michael's eyes twinkled with mischievousness. "Nope. Take it off, Ada. It'll never do. At least until you're thirty." He clicked his tongue and shook his head, holding back a grin. "No, I can't be having my baby girl look like a grown woman."

Ada rolled her eyes. "Oh, Papa, please. It's not a fascinator. It's a bonnet."

Emma burst into laughter, shaking her head playfully. "You two."

Ada's smile turned serious, her eyes sincere. "Thank you for all you've done, Emma. You've been so unselfish and kind, even when I didn't deserve it. The love you've shown me—well, I appreciate it."

Ada's words filled the space—and Emma's heart—carrying with them a profound sense of gratitude. Her eyes met Ada's with gentle affection, mirroring the love that overflowed inside her. "My precious girl, thank you for your gracious words. They mean more to me than you could ever imagine."

Michael sighed, distracting them from the special moment. Emma searched his face for what he thought and found a peacefulness she'd rarely seen. "You girls are going to make me cry."

Emma might just join him. But a little piece of her wondered, would this new Ada last?

By the next day, the worries that had plagued Michael began to fade into the background, replaced by a growing excitement for the intimate moments that awaited him and Emma.

In the stillness of the twilight, Ada joined him on the parapet for an evening of stargazing, as he had promised her. On such a bright and calm evening, he decided to keep the light off until they were done. "I told you we'd share a special evening together, darling. What do you see?"

Ada pointed to the sky. "The big dipper is easy to spot. But can I ask a favor?"

He quirked a brow. "Anything."

"Can Emma join us? It doesn't feel right without her here. Please?"

He couldn't believe his ears. She'd fought to have time alone with him, but now she was begging to include Emma? "Of course, dear girl. Go and fetch her. And ask her to bring some iced tea and cookies too. We can have a little stargazing party."

In a flash, Ada disappeared down the ladder. From the parapet, he watched her scurry inside, and within minutes, she and Emma appeared, cookies and tea in hand. He hurried down the stairs to take the pitcher and glasses, for he knew Emma would struggle carrying them and holding her dress as to not trip on it.

Emma handed him the glasses and pitcher but took the plate of cookies from Ada. "I can manage this. Let's have a parapet party."

As they ascended the spiral staircase, Ada giggled. "I'll show you all the constellations, Emma. I've learned them over the years, you know, and I know them better than any of my classmates. Teacher says I have an eye for the sky."

"That's great, Ada, because I need some lessons." Emma laughed, her cheery voice reverberating on the metal tower walls. "My friend, Laurie Jean, once scolded me for my lack of celestial smarts."

When they reached the parapet, Emma poured them each a glass of tea and handed each of them a cookie. The night sky unfolded before them, a vast canvas of twinkling stars. The cool breeze tousled her hair, and Ada's eyes sparkled with excitement.

She studied the sky and pointed. "Look, Emma. Over there is Orion, the mighty hunter. See those three bright stars in a row? They make up his belt. And if you follow the belt down, you'll see his sword hanging from it."

Emma was clearly captivated by Ada's enthusiastic explanations. "That's incredible, Ada. I've heard of Orion, but I never knew how to identify him in the sky. You truly are an expert."

Ada beamed with pride. "Papa taught me all I know. He's the brilliant one. But thank you. Orion is my favorite constellation. Cassiopeia is my second. See that group of stars over there? It looks like a big M or W depending on how it's positioned."

Emma stared at the sky for several moments

and frowned. Michael helped her to see it by coming behind her and pointing within her field of vision. Finally, she exclaimed, "I see it! I see it, Ada! Show me more."

Ada grinned wide. "Your turn, Papa. I want to eat my cookie."

Michael chuckled. "You can have mine too. You need to put some meat on those bones, my girl."

She rolled her eyes and took a bite while Emma waited expectantly, her gaze trained on the stars. What a glorious night, having both of his girls with him on this perfectly clear, still summer's eve!

He searched for the next constellation he could introduce her to. "Look there, just above the horizon. That is Ursa Major, the Great Bear."

Emma nodded. "I only knew one until now. There . . . those seven stars are the Big Dipper."

Ada clanged her glass on Emma's, almost making her spill it. "Good for you. That's a start. And now you know lots more. Won't your friend be pleased?"

"She will indeed."

The hour slipped away as they immersed themselves in the celestial spectacle above them. They marveled at the beauty of the stars, connecting the dots to form mythical creatures and heroes of ancient tales. Laughter and whispers filled the air, blending with the distant sound of crashing waves.

Suddenly, a streak of light shot across the sky, leaving a trail of shimmering stardust in its wake. The three of them gasped in unison, their eyes fixed on the falling star.

Emma cheered. "Quick, make a wish!"

They all closed their eyes, but Michael peeked at the beauties before him, gazing at their faces illuminated by the starlight, lovelier than the heavens. His breath caught in his throat, and he swallowed several times to dislodge the lump that had settled there.

Ada leaned on the railing and hung, her feet dangling. "I hope my wish comes true. I wished for our family to have more adventures together and create lots of memories."

Emma sighed, her gaze on Ada filled with love. "My wish is for love and happiness to fill our lives, for us to continue growing stronger as a family."

Michael swallowed again. "My wish is for us to remember this night—the beauty of the stars, the joy we feel, and the precious bond that holds us together."

For several minutes, silence settled between them. But then, Emma spoke softly, almost in a whisper. "It's amazing to think how our creator God formed all this—the earth, the stars, us." Her voice reflected reverence he'd rarely experienced, even in church. "And we don't even know how vast the heavens are. Perhaps God is still creating new stars and galaxies, just for fun. Just like I enjoy creating wonderful meals and you creating beautiful pictures, Ada, I think God enjoys creating too. New babies. New flowers and trees. And stars."

Ada glanced at the sky. "Do you think God made all the stars? My science teacher says the stars make other stars, like acorns make trees."

Emma paused, her gaze fixed on the heavens above, as if she was searching for the right words. "Ada, my dear girl, I believe that the universe is like a magnificent work of art, and God is the artist behind it all. Just as a painter meticulously crafts each brushstroke, or a composer weaves together wonderful melodies, I believe that God intricately designed every star, every planet, and every constellation. The Bible says that the heavens declare the glory of God."

Michael added his own perspective. "I agree completely, Emma. And not only did God create this beautiful tapestry of the night sky, but He also gave us the ability to appreciate and wonder at its beauty. Can you feel it? It's as if the stars are whispers from God, inviting us to ponder our place in the world and explore the mysteries that lie beyond."

Emma slipped her hand into his and whispered, "I love you, Michael."

He whispered back. "I love you more, wife."

For a long while, the three of them enjoyed a

sense of wonder, their conversation meandering effortlessly, touching on hopes, dreams, and the beauty they savored. Laughter filled the air as Ada shared some star jokes, as she called them. "Why did the star go to school?"

Emma shrugged. "You stumped me."

Ada chuckled. "To get brighter."

The three of them guffawed for several moments, but she had more.

"Why did the star become an actor?"

Michael shook his head. "I'm not very good at jokes, darlin'."

Ada waved an arm. "It wanted to be in the spotlight."

That yielded mirthful groans.

She put her finger in the air. "One more. Why did the star bring a ladder to the party?"

Emma glanced at him, trying to hold back a laugh. Her eyes danced joyfully. Together, Emma and he shrugged, raising their hands in surrender.

Ada's proud smile lit up the night. "Because it wanted to reach the sky."

They groaned together before chuckling at the answer. Ada always loved jokes and remembered every punch line with perfect precision.

When their laughter subsided, he sighed. "As much as I hate to say it, you'd better get to bed, my sweet Ada girl, and I need to light the lamp. But how about I come and tuck you in? I haven't done that in a while."

"How about you and Emma tuck me in together? I'd like that."

Emma put her hand to her chest, her eyes misting with joy. "I'd like that, too, Ada. I think your papa's wish will come true. I'll always remember this evening and the love we shared. And I won't forget the constellations either. Thanks for the lessons. Your teachers should be proud of you."

Ada shrugged. "They are, 'cept Mr. Perkins, our math teacher. He said my head is full of holes that the numbers slip through. He says girls have no mind for arithmetic."

Michael countered the idea firmly. "That's not true, Ada, and don't you believe it. Your mother was a whiz at numbers. She could do sums faster than the shopkeeper."

Ada smiled. "Then I want to be like my mama. Like Emma and Mama."

Another lump filled his throat. If he weren't careful, he'd become a weeping mess right then and there.

Chapter 16

The next morning, Emma woke up with a sense of excitement bubbling inside her. Today was going to be a special day for father and daughter, a day filled with laughter, adventure, and cherished memories. Michael would soon be done with work, and they would take Ada on one final outing before they sent her off to school.

With a spring in her step, Emma made her way to the kitchen, her mind already filled with thoughts of the delicious breakfast she would prepare. She decided to make scrambled eggs and crispy bacon, a breakfast fit for fishermen. As the eggs sizzled in the pan and the aroma of bacon filled the air, Emma smiled, hoping every bite would be savored by her loved ones.

While the breakfast was cooking, Emma prepared a picnic lunch for Michael and Ada's fishing adventure. She carefully packed sandwiches, slices of cheese and cucumbers, fruit, and some homemade cookies, ensuring that they had everything they would need for a perfect day on the water. She even included a bottle filled with fresh lemonade, knowing Michael and Ada both enjoyed the tasty drink.

Just as Emma was putting the finishing

touches on the picnic basket, hurrying footsteps approached the kitchen. Ada bounced in, her face brimming with anticipation and happiness. Her eyes sparkled with excitement as she clutched a small fishing net.

Michael came in from his night watch and planted a tender kiss on Emma's cheek. "Good morning, ladies. Ready to go fishing, Ada?"

Emma closed the lid on the picnic basket. "Good morning, family. Breakfast is almost ready, and I've packed a delicious picnic lunch for you to enjoy later."

Michael smiled as he sat down and sipped the coffee Emma put before him. "Thanks, wife. You keep us well fed. I'll miss you today, but I'm sure we'll bring a stringer of fish for us all to enjoy."

As they gathered around the kitchen table, Emma served the breakfast, placing steaming plates in front of Michael and Ada. They dug in eagerly, savoring each bite and exchanging glances of delight between mouthfuls.

Emma gazed at Ada with an indulgent smile. "It's so good to see you eating well, Ada."

Before responding, Ada patted her lips like a little lady. "You're a good cook, Emma."

While they ate, Michael and Ada discussed their fishing plans. Emma had planned to spend the day catching up on laundry, but she listened to Ada's excitement and infectious enthusiasm, wishing she could join them. Still, this was their special father-daughter outing, and she'd not want to intrude.

Halfway through the breakfast, Ada glanced at her and smiled. "Emma, would you come fishing with us today? It would be so much fun, and we can all enjoy this special day together."

Emma's heart swelled with love for the little girl maturing into a young lady. She looked at Michael, who nodded in agreement, his eyes filled with gratitude and warmth.

The laundry could wait. This was a chance for them to create beautiful memories as a family. "I was just wishing I could join you, but I didn't want to intrude on your father-daughter time. Are you sure?"

Ada nodded, heartily chewing a fatty piece of bacon.

Michael nodded enthusiastically, winking his approval. His gaze darted between her and Ada, then he threw back his head and cheered. "Let's make this a day to remember, family!"

With that decision made, they finished their breakfast, cleared the table, and gathered their fishing gear, ready to embark on their trip. Emma added another serving of lunch to the picnic basket, and they were ready.

Hand in hand, they walked toward the skiff, the picnic basket swinging gently on Emma's arm. She'd only been fishing a few times, and none in the past few years, so a little apprehension niggled at her. But being with her family set those worries aside.

As they eased out into the St. Lawrence, she wondered where they would go. She really didn't care, but she'd rarely been able to explore the river with its many islands and inlets. Perhaps Michael and she could make that a regular adventure, at least until the winter winds blew.

They began their day of fishing just downriver between Mandolin and Cedar islands. "Walleye love it here," Michael explained as he dropped anchor. "Bullheads too."

They cast their lines into the water, hoping for a successful catch. But luck wasn't on their side, and they only managed to catch a few small fish, which they promptly released back into the river. Michael waved them off. "Let's let them grow a little more. There are plenty of big fish in the river."

For a long while, Emma simply watched them. But finally, she couldn't resist the call of the river herself. With a smile, she grabbed a fishing rod and joined Michael and Ada. Time seemed to stand still as they immersed themselves in the tranquility of the moment. The gentle lapping of the water against the boat and the distant call of seagulls created a serene atmosphere.

Ada's laughter echoed through the air every time she caught a glimpse of a fish swimming beneath the surface. Michael patiently taught both Emma and Ada the art of angling, showing them how to cast the line and wait for a bite. Emma watched with delight as Ada's eyes lit up with excitement and wonder, her small hands gripping the fishing rod with determination.

The St. Lawrence River stretched out before them, its waters shimmering with the golden rays of the sun. The lush greenery of the islands provided a picturesque backdrop, and the fresh scent of the river mingled with the gentle breeze. She soaked in the peaceful ambiance and warmth of the sun on her skin. It was a moment of pure bliss, a chance to escape the worries of everyday life and simply be present in the beauty of nature.

Ada grew frustrated with her lack of catches, and her voice turned whiny. "We aren't catching much, Papa."

Michael straightened, his mouth flattening into a firm line. "You're right, darlin'. Let's head up to Susan and Frederick islands and make our way down to Orient and Rylestone islands. Then maybe we'll end up at Reed Point before heading home. How does that sound?"

Ada nodded, and Emma shrugged. "I've heard of those islands, but you're the expert. Carry on, then."

They set off, the boat gliding across the calm river surface, and soon they arrived at Frederick Island.

To their delight, the fish were biting furiously.

Michael caught a largemouth bass, and Ada managed to reel in four perch. Emma tried, too, but both times she got a bite, the fish managed to escape.

Emma laughed, lowering her pole to the keel. "I think I'll retire from fishing for today. I'd rather enjoy the company and the views."

She leaned back, taking in the breathtaking scenery around them. She basked in the joy of being surrounded by her loved ones. They told stories, laughed, and even engaged in some friendly competition. Michael and Ada took turns casting their lines, hoping to reel in a prized catch, and Ada took the gold. A large northern pike latched onto her line and wouldn't let go. But tenacious Ada wouldn't let go either. In the end, Michael had to help her pull in what had to be a nine pounder. They'd be eating on it for days!

The hours drifted by, and the picnic lunch that Emma had prepared beckoned them. With excitement, they stopped at one of the tiny islands south of Rhylestone and gathered around the basket, savoring the sandwiches, fruits, and homemade cookies. The flavors mingled with the fresh, crisp air, adding to the magic of the day.

As the outing neared its end and the sun dipped low on the horizon, casting a golden glow over the river, they knew it was time to bid farewell to their fishing haven. The catch of the day might not have been the most significant part of their adventure, for the bonds they had strengthened and the joy they had experienced were far more precious.

Michael skillfully guided the skiff back to Rock Island as a sense of exhaustion settled on them all. Ada's eyes grew heavy, and Emma watched with contentment and fondness as the child drifted off to sleep, still clutching her fishing net tightly.

The day had been about so much more than just angling or catching fish. It had been about building memories, strengthening their bond as a family, and cherishing the simple joys that life had to offer. Emma would forever hold dear the memories they had created and the peace they had found in each other's company.

How could she say goodbye to the little girl who had become the center of their world?

The next morning, Michael, Emma, and Ada made their way to the quaint Thousand Island Park chapel for the Sunday service. The members of the community had been a pillar of support during Ada's illness, praying for her recovery and encouraging Michael when he visited the shops.

As they walked from the dock to the church, Ada tugged them along. "Hurry, Papa and Emma. Mary and her aunts will be there, and I can't wait to see her."

Emma smiled. "Do you know that Mary's aunts held prayer gatherings when you were sick?"

Ada placed a palm on her chest. "For me?"

He agreed. "For you. This community cares for you. For us."

When they entered the chapel, the atmosphere was filled with a joyous anticipation. Once they settled into their seats, those nearby greeted them warmly, their smiles reflecting the happiness they felt upon seeing Ada healthy and well once again.

Throughout the service, whispers of joy rippled through the pews when people caught glimpses of Ada. As the service came to a close, the congregation rose to sing a hymn of thanksgiving, melodic voices filling the chapel. Michael and his little family joined in.

After the service, as they made their way toward the door, they were met with a flood of well-wishers. Members of the congregation approached them, their eyes filled with tears of joy as they expressed heartfelt concern.

"Ada, my dear, we are so grateful to see you well!" Mr. Wiseman's voice trembled with emotion as he hugged her. "May God bless you as you return to school."

Michael shook his hand. "Thanks for your prayers. I know they made a difference."

One by one, people approached Ada, embracing her and expressing their happiness at her recovery. Ada listened intently, her smile beaming at the affection and attention. Michael stood between Ada and his wife, his heart overflowing with gratitude for the outpouring of love and support.

As they made their way outside, Emma shifted her gloves from one hand to the other. "I hadn't realized how much Ada's journey touched the hearts of these people."

Joy welled up inside him. "Indeed, we are truly blessed to have such caring individuals in our lives."

Ada frowned. "I'll miss them too. But where are Mary and her aunts?"

Emma put her hand over her brow to shield her eyes from the sun and scan the crowd. "I just saw them at the back of the church but haven't seen them since."

Just then, Mary rounded the corner with sparkling eyes and a small bouquet of wildflowers in her hand. "I picked these for you, but Aunt Stella was feeling poorly, so they went home. I can't stay, but Auntie said you're leaving for school? I am, too, and I'm going to miss you."

Ada's eyes teared up. She hugged Mary tightly, promising to stay in touch and to never forget the special time they shared. "Write me, will you?"

Mary clung to both of Ada's hands. "I'll write if you'll write me back. But don't be sad. We'll see each other next summer. We can be pen pals until then."

Ada giggled. "That'll be wonderful, Mary. See

you next summer." They exchanged one final gaze, their eyes speaking volumes of unspoken words—love, friendship, and a promise to cherish the memories they had created.

Michael cleared his throat. "Ready for lunch? Rob said Laurie Jean ran home early. And she's made a feast."

When they arrived at Laurie Jean and Robert's quaint little cottage and settled down for a delightful lunch, Ada asked, "Do you have kids?"

Laurie Jean beamed. "Three, but they're grown up and live far from here. My daughter lives in Rochester, and she just had our first grandchild. I'm going to see them later this week."

Ada's eyes sparked with interest, and she grinned. "I'm going there, too, this week. Maybe we can take the train together."

Laurie Jean's face lit up. "That'd be wonderful. I don't like traveling, but Robert has to work."

Robert leaned forward. "It would be a pleasure to have you travel with her, Ada."

Ada waved a hand. "I like traveling. Trains are fun, and I'm used to going alone since Papa has to work."

Michael exchanged a grateful glance with Emma. He turned to Laurie Jean. "Thank you for your kind offer. It gives me peace for you to accompany Ada on this trip."

With the plans set in motion, Michael would telegram his mother to share the news. He'd always hated letting Ada go alone, but he couldn't leave the light untended that long, and he fretted until he received a telegram from his mother telling him she was safe and sound. His heart lightened knowing his girl would be looked after on her journey to school.

As the lunch continued, they discussed the logistics of the trip, and Ada offered suggestions for the best places Laurie Jean might want to visit in Rochester. He chuckled at his only child. Her confidence always amazed him.

Overflowing with gratitude, he raised his glass, proposing a toast to the upcoming journey. "To new adventures and cherished friendships." The clink of glasses resonated through the dining room, sealing the promise of a pleasant journey for Ada.

When they returned to Rock Island, dusk was already settling in, and the fireflies were out in abundance.

"Can we catch some lightning bugs, please? I haven't had a firefly lantern all summer." Ada feigned a little-girl pout. She stuck her bottom lip out and batted her eyes. "Pretty please?"

He and Emma laughed at her antics. "You may. Give me a few minutes to light the lamp, and then I'll join you and Emma in the fun."

Ada hugged him tightly. "Oh, thank you. I'm not even a little tired."

Emma took her hand. "You may feel fine now,

but you still have to rest often, especially when you're at school. School will have long, grueling days, and we wouldn't want you to get ill."

Ada scrunched up her nose. "Oh, you don't have to worry. Granny makes me go to bed at seven o'clock every night."

Emma chuckled. "I can't wait to meet your granny, sweetheart. But for now, let's find a canning jar and make a firefly lantern. I made one every summer when I was a child."

When Michael returned to the lawn, he was greeted by a scene that filled his heart with happiness. Ada's infectious joy overflowed as she caught fireflies that danced around her, gently cupping them in her hands and releasing them into the jar-turned-lantern that Emma held for her, where they bathed the glass with their ethereal glow.

Emma observed Ada with a soft smile.

Michael winked at Emma, caught a firefly, and planted a playful kiss on the tip of her nose. "The fireflies look beautiful in the jar, but not as pretty as you."

After Michael deposited his firefly in the jar, Ada took it from Emma, holding it close to her chest. The fireflies illuminated the darkness, creating a mesmerizing dance of light that captivated all of them.

He reached out and gently ruffled Ada's hair, a gesture filled with affection. "You know, Ada, the fireflies are like little stars you've captured. I think God put lightning bugs here not only to illuminate the night but also to bring a touch of magic into our lives."

Emma clasped her hands against her chest. "They are magical. But you two have lit up my life in ways I never could have imagined."

Michael wrapped her in a hug. "So have you, Emma."

To his surprise, Ada joined them in a group hug. Could he ask for a sweeter close to their summer?

Chapter 17

The next morning, as the sun peeked through the curtains, Emma rose from her bed with a heavy heart. Today she would have to start packing Ada's things in her trunk. The thought of sending her off to school, hours away from home, filled her with surprising melancholy. Just weeks ago, she'd dreaded the days of conflict and troubles. Now, she was sad to see Ada go.

Yet, with each passing day, Ada's excitement had grown, and she had become increasingly restless. It seemed that Ada lived in two worlds—the one here at Rock Island Lighthouse and the other in Rochester with her granny and schoolmates. Ada missed her friends, and the prospect of seeing them again filled her with joy. She missed her granny too.

Emma carefully folded Ada's neatly pressed dresses and placed them inside the trunk. She recalled the countless hours she had spent nursing Ada back to health. The ups and downs. The friction and fun. Ada's interest in God and the transformation Emma had witnessed. So many memories in just one, life-changing summer.

She glanced up from the trunk as Michael entered the room and immediately recognized anxiousness etched across his face, mirroring the emotions she had been grappling with herself. How much would Ada change while she was away? Would their relationship remain strong? Her leaving was indeed bittersweet.

She set aside the dress she was folding and walked over to Michael, placing a comforting hand on his arm. "It's hard, isn't it?" Her voice caught in her throat. "Does it ever get easier?"

Michael sighed deeply and shook his head, his eyes fixed on the floor. "I'm afraid not, Emma. I'm proud of Ada's independence and eagerness to learn, but I still don't like it when she leaves."

She squeezed his arm gently, understanding his sadness all too well. "Though I've known her only this short time, I feel the same way. I'm sure it's natural for us to worry about her safety and well-being. But we have to trust in God and hope the values you've instilled in her will stand the test of time. She's responsible and resourceful, and she's proven time and time again that she can navigate the world with confidence."

He looked into her eyes, gratitude shining through his worry. "She is confident, that's for sure. And independent."

She gave him her warmest smile. "This is her chance to grow, to gain new experiences and friendships. As much as it pains us to see her go, we must support her."

He let out a heavy sigh and wrapped his arms around her, clearly seeking strength in her embrace. "You're right, and you being here makes it a little easier. We'll always be here for her every step of the way, even if it's from a distance."

She hugged him tightly. "We'll write her letters, send her our love and support. And when she comes back home during breaks, we'll cherish every moment with her. Our girl may be venturing out into the world, but she'll always have her family waiting with open arms."

Michael's eyes twinkled. "And in between, I'll get to hold you in my arms."

She giggled. "And so much more."

An hour later, when the three of them sat down for lunch, their varied emotions swirled in the air. Ada chattered excitedly about reuniting with her classmates, describing the adventures they would have and the lessons they would learn together. Her enthusiasm was contagious, and despite their anxiety, Emma and Michael couldn't help but smile at her renewed energy.

Emma's eyes misted. "Seeing you healthy and embracing the world fills my heart with immense happiness. This summer has been truly amazing, but I must admit, I'll miss having you around the cottage. These walls will feel empty without your laughter and curious questions."

Ada took her hand, squeezing it gently. "I'll miss you, too, Emma. But I promise to write you letters regularly, sharing all the exciting things happening at school."

For the next two days, Emma busied herself with last-minute preparations. She sewed nametags onto Ada's clothes, ensuring that nothing would be lost or misplaced in the bustling school environment. She packed a small box of homemade treats, knowing that Ada would appreciate a taste of home during her time away.

On the morning before Ada left for school, Emma sat on the porch, darning one of Ada's socks. The sun bathed the world in a warm glow, but inside her, a variety of emotions churned. She sensed Ada's restlessness as the girl aimlessly hopped from step to step, stopping to gaze at Emma, then repeating her zigzag pattern. Emma set aside her darning and turned her attention fully to her.

"What is it, darling?" She met Ada's troubled gaze. "I can tell you're just aching to ask me something."

Ada stood before her and fidgeted, her fingers tracing the edge of her skirt. "I am. Why . . . why do you call me your daughter?" She finally managed to ask her question, her voice filled with a blend of curiosity and vulnerability.

Emma's heart skipped a beat at the inquiry. She hadn't anticipated this particular question, but she understood the significance behind it. She patted the empty space beside her, inviting Ada to sit down. Once they were side by side, Emma took a deep breath, gathering her thoughts.

"Ada, sweetheart," she said with tenderness, "family is not just about blood. It's about the love and connection we share, the bonds we form through care and support. From the moment your father and I fell in love, I knew that you were an important part of his life, and by extension, an important part of mine."

Ada looked at her, her surprise evident.

Emma continued. "Calling you my daughter is my way of expressing the love and affection I have for you. It's a way of acknowledging the special place you hold in my heart, regardless of the fact that we don't share a biological connection."

Tears filled the child's eyes. "Thank you, but I do still miss my mama."

She reached out to gently hold Ada's hand. "I'm sure you do, darling, and I'm not trying to replace her. She'll always be your mama, and you'll always love and miss her, as you should. But being a mother is not just about giving birth to someone. It's about nurturing, guiding, and supporting them in their journey through life. It's about being there through the ups and downs, celebrating their successes and offering a comforting presence during their challenges. And that's what I want to do for you, Ada."

Ada's grip on her hand tightened slightly. "But what if I'm not like your real daughter? What if I disappoint you?"

Emma's heart ached at her words, and she leaned closer, wrapping her arm around her. "Ada, listen to me. You are not a disappointment. Never will be. You are a remarkable girl, full of potential and strength. You bring joy, laughter, and love into our lives. The love I have for you is unconditional, birthed from God's love. You are my daughter in every sense of the word."

Ada sniffled, leaning into her embrace. "Thank you, Emma," she whispered. "I'm grateful you are in my life, even if we're not related by blood."

"And I'm grateful to have you in my life, Ada." She held the child tightly, her tone filled with love and compassion. "Never doubt the love and support your father and I have for you. No matter what challenges lie ahead, we'll face them together, as a family."

Michael stood in the dimly lit lamp room, the flickering remnants of the lantern's flame casting eerie shadows on the walls. The weight of the impending farewell settled heavily in his heart. Ada stood on the precipice of another year away from him. The time had come for her to return to school.

It was their last day together, so he decided to take Ada and Emma to Thousand Island Park and have lunch at the Columbian Hotel. An extravagant treat, but well worth it. And he'd ask Mr. Wiseman to join them.

When he announced his plan to Emma, she kissed him. "What a wonderful idea! Let's make one more special memory with her."

Ada, too, was excited, though a little less so without her friend, Mary, who had already returned to Watertown. "Can I wear my flower girl dress and new bonnet?"

Emma nodded. "I'll dress up too."

Michael held up his finger. "Me too. Be back in a jiffy, ladies." He playfully ran to the stairs and bounded up them two at a time, well ahead of Emma and Ada. "Beat you!" he teased.

Emma and Ada rolled their eyes at his silliness but hurried to get dressed. He donned his best Sunday suit, shaved, and added an extra dab of cologne.

Before long, they set off for Thousand Island Park in the skiff. Upon reaching the shore, they strolled along St. Lawrence Avenue, hand in hand, the summer sunshine enveloping them in a comforting embrace. But the breeze was a little crisp, carrying with it the whispers of change and the promise of new beginnings.

Soon, they arrived at the grand Columbian Hotel, a place full of memories. Inside, the ambience was refined, with crystal chandeliers casting a soft glow over the exquisite dining room. His heart swelled as he led his wife and daughter to their table, eagerly awaiting the arrival of their dear friend and mentor, Mr. Wiseman.

When he arrived, they exchanged greetings and settled into an animated conversation, their laughter mingling with the clinking of fine china. The older man gave Emma a note from Laurie Jean saying that she and Robert would meet them at the train station tomorrow, promptly at ten. Plans finalized, they'd enjoy the day.

Over a sumptuous meal, they reminisced about Ada's summer, sharing stories of her insatiable appetite for knowledge and her unwavering determination, even in the face of scarlet fever.

Mr. Wiseman leaned forward. "Michael, my friend, Ada is a remarkable girl. Sending her off to school is the greatest gift you can give her."

He nodded, glanced at Ada, and smiled. "I know, but it's hard to let go. She's such a joy to our world." He turned to his daughter, taking her hand. "No matter the distance between us, our love will always surround you."

Ada nodded. "Emma said that too. I know, Papa."

As the afternoon waned, they bid Mr. Wiseman farewell. The gentleman embraced Ada tightly, imparting a prayer and well wishes.

The day had been a bittersweet blend of joy and sadness, and Michael found himself unwilling to let it end. He wanted to savor every remaining moment with Ada.

As they climbed into the skiff, he suggested, "Why don't we take the long way back? We can weave through the islands and make this day last a little longer."

Ada's face lit up, mirroring his sentiment. "That sounds wonderful, Papa. I'd love to explore the islands one last time."

Emma voiced her apprehension, cocking her head at him. "Are you certain, sweetheart? It will be quite a long row back, and the sun will set in a few hours. Besides, you have a full night ahead of you."

He turned to her, his heart tender and determined. "I want to make the most of this day. We'll be fine. I promise. And besides, it will give us some extra time to make plans to see Ada at Christmas."

Emma nodded, her trust in his judgment unwavering.

She and Ada settled onto the seat facing him, and Michael took up the oars. He navigated the skiff between the islands, the oars cutting through the water with a steady rhythm, propelling them past tiny Hub Island and Pullman Island.

"Papa, do you remember the time we picnicked on Pullman Island? We spent hours exploring and finding hidden treasures." A wistful smile graced her lips.

He chuckled, his gaze fixed on the distant horizon. "Of course, darling. We found shells, flat rocks for skipping, and even a message in a bottle. Those were magical moments, weren't they?"

"Yes, they were."

The conversation turned to plans for the Christmas holidays as they made their way through the narrow passage between Castle Francis Island and Twin Island.

"Ada, it'll be so good to see your world and meet your grandmother." Emma's voice danced with excitement. "I haven't been to Rochester, so you'll have to be my tour guide, okay?"

Ada nodded. "I can't wait. I'll show you everything, and you'll love Granny. It will be wonderful to see you then."

While the sky painted itself in hues of gold and rose, the journey neared its end. The skiff glided to a gentle halt on the dock of Rock Island. Ada tugged him into an impulsive hug. "Thank you, Papa, for this magical day. I'll treasure it always."

Emma brushed a stray lock of hair from her face. "We will, too, sweetheart."

As the sun dipped below the horizon, casting a final golden glow over the water, they turned toward the cottage. Ada ran ahead, so he slipped his arm around Emma's waist and pulled her close. "And we'll make some magic days of our own, won't we, wife?"

Chapter 18

The morning sun filtered through the gauzy curtains, casting a warm glow across the room where Emma stood buttoning Ada's dress. Today, Ada was setting off on her journey, one filled with excitement for the girl, yet tinged with a subtle wistfulness for Emma. With each button secured through its loop, she felt as if a small part of Ada was slipping away, growing up and venturing out into a world that Emma herself had seldom dared to explore.

"There. All ready to travel." Emma adjusted Ada's collar with a gentle touch to ensure everything was perfect. "I'm so glad Laurie Jean will travel with you." A smile played at the corners of her lips as she leaned closer with playful secrecy. "And I'll tell you a little secret . . ." She cupped her hands around Ada's ear, creating a bit of conspiracy. "Laurie Jean was scared to travel alone. You rescued her. Thanks."

Ada's reaction was immediate and delightful. "I rescued a grownup? Goodness!"

Emma straightened Ada's bonnet, her hands lingering a moment longer than necessary, not quite ready to let go. "You did. Most people aren't as frequent a traveler as you are. I'm certainly not. I've rarely traveled. Not like you."

Ada's chest swelled with responsibility. "I'll take good care of her, I promise." She paused, a sudden seriousness replacing her earlier excitement. She took a deep breath, her gaze flitting around the room as if she was searching for the right words, or perhaps for courage.

Emma recognized that look. "A penny for your thoughts, darling?"

Ada hesitated, her hand moving almost unconsciously to her mouth, a nervous habit she had picked up from who knew where as she clutched the fabric of her skirt. "I've been thinking . . . a lot, actually. About families."

Emma nodded, encouraging her to continue. "What about families, Ada?"

"Well, everyone has a mama, right? And they call her 'mother'?" Ada's eyes searched Emma's, looking for confirmation.

"That's true for a lot of people, yes." Emma spoke gently, aware of the complexities her answer held.

Ada bit her lip, hesitating. "Do you think . . . I mean, would it be all right if . . . if I called you 'Mother'?"

The question hung in the air, a fragile bubble that Emma feared to burst with even the slightest breath. Time seemed to slow as emotions rushed over her, each one colliding with the next—surprise, joy, fear, and an overwhelming sense of love. She had cared for Ada all summer, through her illness, watching over her with all the tenderness of a mother, yet without the title. And frankly, she didn't expect it.

Kneeling down to Ada's level, Emma took the girl's hands in hers, her heart swelling as she looked into Ada's earnest, hopeful eyes. "Ada, my dearest girl," Emma began, her voice soft but steady. "You calling me 'Mother' would make me very happy. But I want to make sure you know what that means to me."

Ada nodded eagerly, leaning in.

"It means that next to God and your father, you are the most important person in my life. It means we are family, not just because we live together, but because we choose each other, care for each other, and support each other. And that's for our whole, entire life, no matter what."

Ada's face lit up with understanding and joy. "I choose you, Emma. And I hope you will choose me too. So can I start now? Can I call you 'Mother' right now . . . and always?"

Emma laughed, a sound rich with happiness, and pulled Ada into a warm embrace. "Yes, my darling Ada. Nothing in the world would make me happier!"

Ada's arms flew around Emma's neck in a fierce, tight hug that spoke volumes. In that moment, as Emma held her close, she realized that Ada's journey wouldn't just be about the miles she would travel, but about the paths they would forge together as a family.

Emma's heart swelled with love for her daughter. *Her* daughter. She squeezed Ada gently, cherishing the moment and the depth of their connection.

"Ada," Emma whispered into her ear, "I am so grateful to have you as my daughter. You are a precious gift, a shining light in my life. It's my greatest joy to love and support you, to be there for you every step of the way. Together, we'll continue to discover the beauty and wonder of God's love."

Ada pulled back to gaze at her as she absorbed her words. There was a sense of curiosity and wonder in her expression, as if a door to a new understanding had been opened.

"You see, Ada, I believe God created me to be part of your life, to listen to your joys and sorrows, and to offer my support in any way I can. His wisdom and compassion will guide me, helping me navigate the beautiful journey of being your mother. We are a family united by God's love, and together, we will always support and care for one another. Your presence fills our home with joy and love, and you bring light and happiness into our lives. But most of all, I consider you to be the greatest gift your father has ever given me."

Ada's hand reached out, finding its way into Emma's, their fingers intertwining in a tender moment. The connection between them was palpable, a demonstration of the bond they enjoyed.

"And I'm so grateful to have you as my mother, Emma . . . I mean . . . Mother."

Emma smiled, her heart overflowing with love and pride. She gently gathered Ada into her arms, enveloping her in another hug. She kissed her on the top of her head before releasing her. "Why don't you finish packing while I get breakfast ready? It'll be time to head to Clayton soon."

Ada smiled. "Yes, *Mother*."

Emma giggled. "I like the sound of that."

She headed downstairs to prepare the morning meal, her heart so light she thought she could fly. *She called me Mother.*

Before long, Emma had the coffee brewing and oatmeal cooking. She cheerfully set the table for breakfast, her movements more buoyant than usual. She placed three bowls on the table, along with spoons, and a small pitcher of milk as her thoughts wandered to the day she had first met Ada, the feisty, angry child who didn't want her around.

"Mother . . ." The word echoed in her ears, a sweet sound that enveloped her with an indescribable warmth. She smiled to herself, a tear of joy threatening to escape. It was a title she had never expected to wear, yet now, it seemed as if the past months of quiet dedication had been leading to this precious moment.

Ada came bouncing down the stairs, her travel case handle gripped firmly in her hand. "All packed!" she announced proudly, placing the case by the door.

At the same time, Michael came through the back door wearing a frown that resembled Ada's when she pouted. He gave Ada and herself a warm hug before taking his seat. "Good morning, ladies."

"Perfect timing." Emma gestured toward the table. "Let's have some breakfast before we leave for Clayton. You need a good meal for the journey, Ada, and I packed a lunch for you and Laurie Jean to share. She probably did, too, so you'll have an abundance."

As they sat down, Ada's eyes were bright. "I can't wait to ride the train with Laurie Jean and maybe even show her around Rochester."

Emma nodded, passing Ada a bowl of oatmeal. She poured some milk into it and then added a generous spoonful of honey and a sprinkle of cinnamon, just the way Ada liked it.

"Eat up," Emma encouraged, her heart swelling with satisfaction as Ada stirred the oatmeal. "You'll need your energy."

"Thank you, Mother," Ada said, and this time, the word flowed more naturally, more confidently.

She smiled at Ada, her heart bursting with affection and gratitude. She reached across the table, squeezing Ada's hand gently. "You're very welcome, my darling daughter."

Michael grinned at them. "What's this I hear?"

Emma opened her mouth to enlighten him, but Ada beat her to it. "I asked Emma if I could call her 'Mother,' and she said yes! I hope that's okay with you, Papa."

He threw back his head and laughed. "Of course, it's okay with me. In fact, that's the best news I've heard in a while."

Indeed, it was. Even though Ada was going away to school, their family was complete.

Mother . . . At first, Michael thought he must have misheard. He had hoped and prayed for Ada to warm up to Emma since their union had begun with all its understandable hesitations and adjustments. But to hear Ada use such an endearing term was more than he had dared to hope for.

As he sat there, momentarily frozen by the affectionate moniker, Ada smiled at Emma. She smiled back, reflecting a mutual affection that was palpable in the room. Emma glanced up and caught his eye, her look conveying the joy that mirrored his own.

His heart swelled with gratitude. He took a bite of his oatmeal, the simple flavors somehow tasting richer than usual. As Ada continued to chat animatedly about plans for the day, his mind replayed the moment she called Emma "Mother" over and over. It was a significant milestone, evidence of the strong bond that had formed despite their rocky start.

Underneath the table, he reached for Emma's hand, giving it a gentle squeeze. She responded with a soft smile, her eyes sparkling with unshed tears of happiness. God had begun to weave their new family closer.

Yet melancholy threatened to dampen his delight, for the day had finally arrived when his beloved daughter would board a train that would take her several hours away. How quickly time had passed, transforming a little girl who was once determined to make Emma's life miserable into a young lady who accepted her as part of the family.

The aroma of freshly baked bread wafted through the air, mingling with the scent of strong coffee. He took a whiff. "Did you make bread this morning?"

Emma nodded. "Sourdough. It rose all night and should be ready in five minutes. I thought we could enjoy some while it's hot, so that the butter melts into little puddles and tastes extra good."

Ada giggled. "Yes! Granny's cook never lets me eat the bread hot out of the oven."

Emma's eyes twinkled as she got up and checked the oven. She pulled out two golden-brown loaves and popped them out of the pans. She carefully sliced the hot bread, the crunch of the crust the only sound in the room. She slathered the slices liberally with fresh butter and handed thick slices to both of them.

"Yum! Thanks, Mother." Ada took a big bite, closed her eyes, and moaned.

He looked up to heaven. *Thanks, God!*

After breakfast, they were soon on their way to the Clayton train station. As they traveled, Ada sat between Emma and him in the wagon with Midnight safe and secure in a crate at her feet. He listened intently while she shared more of her dreams and aspirations, and he encouraged her to pursue them wholeheartedly. "You can do anything you put your mind to, my sweet girl. Be good for Granny and learn well."

Emma added, "And keep close to God, okay?"

Ada smiled. "I will. I've learned a lot about Him this summer, and I'll take it with me."

What more could he ask for? His heart overflowed with appreciation—for God, for Emma, for Ada, and even for the lessons learned through Ada's illness.

When they arrived at the train station, the platform was filled with bustling travelers, suitcases in hand, bidding farewell to their loved ones. Ada clutched Michael's and Emma's hands, her excitement—and a touch of nervousness—evident.

Emma fought back tears as she looked at him. This was the beginning of a new chapter in their lives. He and Emma would be alone, learning to navigate married life without Ada. How would that work? He'd figure that out soon enough.

He hugged Ada and promised to write her letters, sharing stories of their daily lives and sending words of encouragement.

"Hello, fellow traveler!" Laurie Jean waved a greeting with Robert close behind, her plump carpetbag in his hand. "Are you ready for our adventure together?" Her voice quivered with nervousness.

Robert set down the bag and shook Michael's hand. "We probably should have come here together, but I have a meeting with the banker at eleven. I didn't want you to have to sit around waiting for me."

"We'd have been happy to tarry here in Clayton, but that's fine. How are you going to manage without your wonderful wife around?" He glanced at the two women who were already busy chatting, Ada holding firmly onto Emma's hand.

Robert shrugged. "I don't cook a lick, but she left me with several meals for this week. After that, I'll probably frequent the diner."

"We'll have you over to Rock Island for a meal or two, just you mind that." Michael took out his pocket watch and checked the time. "We'd better get the train tickets and hand in the luggage."

He and Robert did just that, leaving the women

to chat as if they'd never see one another again. When he returned, Michael cleared the lump in his throat. "I'm sad to say that it's time to go. Remember, my sweet Ada, God is with you, and we can't wait to see the incredible things you'll achieve."

Ada flung her arms around him. "Thank you, Papa, for everything. I love you and Mother so much."

"We love you, too, Ada." His voice trembled as he hugged Ada one last time. "More than words can express. Go out there and make us proud."

Michael felt a familiar tightening in his chest as Ada stepped up into the train with Midnight in his crate, her figure dwarfed by the imposing steel beast that was about to carry her away.

Emma, ever the rock in moments like these, called out with a cheerfulness she might not have truly felt. "Have fun! We love you!" Her voice carried over the clamor, a lifeline thrown across the increasing distance.

Ada's hand pressed against her window, her mouth moving in a silent echo of Emma's words. As the train gave a lurching start, Michael's heart hitched. He waved and blew kisses, every muscle in his body willing the train to stay just a moment longer. Beside him, Emma slipped her hand into his, giving it a reassuring squeeze while Robert waved goodbye to his wife.

As the train gathered speed, Michael's gaze

remained fixed on the window where Ada had stood. Even as she disappeared from view, his eyes stayed locked on that point, as if he could will the connection to remain tangible. He whispered a silent prayer, his words a soft murmur lost in the rush of the departing train. "Keep her safe, Lord, and let her thrive."

The platform now felt emptier, the noise hollow without Ada's vibrant presence. Michael remained rooted in place, emotions brewing inside him—sadness at her departure, pride in her growing independence, and a poignant sense of letting go. Emma stood by him.

As the last train car vanished, Michael finally allowed himself to relax slightly, the initial pang of separation easing into a quiet acceptance. Turning to Emma and Robert, he offered a small, hopeful smile. "She's going to do great things," he said, more to reassure himself than anyone else.

After bidding Robert farewell, he and Emma walked back to the wagon, the cool morning air brisk against their faces. When they climbed into the wagon, Michael turned to Emma and smiled. "And now, my dearest wife, how about we go home and write the next chapter of our journey?"

Emma leaned into him and sighed. "Let's."

Chapter 19

In the days that followed, Emma discovered that she and Michael would have a thriving marriage after all, fueled by his unwavering support and affection.

At first, the sudden freedom of having the house to themselves felt a bit . . . strange. She had grown accustomed to Ada's presence and the responsibilities that came with her. Yet on that first morning after Ada left, Michael came in from his work and sat with her on the porch, sipping tea in comfortable silence. He reached over and gently squeezed her hand, a mischievous glint in his eye. "You know, my dear," he murmured, "now that we have the house to ourselves, we can . . . do anything we want."

A familiar sensation fluttered in her chest, accompanied by a rush of warmth that she hadn't felt in quite some time.

He leaned in, his lips brushing against her ear.

"And what, pray tell, did you have in mind?" she asked, her voice low and playful.

He chuckled, the sound music to her ears. "Well, to start, we could go for a stroll, hand-in-hand, as we used to when we were first courting."

She chuckled, the tension in her shoulders melting away. "Sounds good."

As they wandered the familiar paths around their home, the awkwardness seemed to lift, replaced by a giddy sense of freedom. When they paused beneath the shady trees, Michael pulled her close, and she quivered at his closeness. While the afternoon wore on, they found themselves wrapped in each other's arms, content in the knowledge that they had all the time in the world to simply be.

"I've missed this," Emma murmured.

Michael pressed a gentle kiss to the top of her head. "Me, too, my love. But I have a feeling that with Ada back at school, we're going to have many opportunities to enjoy the belated honeymoon season we need."

Emma smiled, snuggling a little closer. "I can't wait. Don't get me wrong—I adore Ada with all my heart. But it will be so nice to have this time to simply be together, without the demands of parenthood constantly pulling us in different directions."

Michael nodded, his free hand coming up to gently caress her cheek. "I feel the same way. We've been so focused on Ada this summer that sometimes I fear I neglected the most important relationship on this earth—the one between us. And I'm sorry for that, dearest."

Emma squeezed his hand, her throat constricting. "Thank you for that, Michael. This summer hasn't been easy, but we got through it, and look at us now. Ada is happy in school, and she calls me 'Mother.' What more could I ask for?"

"Me, my dearest wife. My undivided attention. My time and love and the opportunity to give you everything you need. That's what you deserve, and that's what I plan to give to you. Every day."

Emma's heart soared at his words.

And in the days and weeks that followed, Michael made it his mission to shower her with love and affirmation. He reminded her daily of her unique qualities, celebrating her victories, comforting her in moments of doubt, and cherishing the essence of who she was. Thanks to his consistent demonstrations of love and acceptance, she slowly started to shed the shackles of self-doubt. She realized that her worth was not defined by past rejections or perceived flaws. Her deepening faith in God and the love she shared with Michael made all the difference.

Ada remained an important focus of their lives, and her letters became a treasure trove of news. Each missive that arrived was thicker than the last, filled with tales of school life that made Emma feel as if she were walking the halls alongside her.

Ada wrote of her classes with tangible enthusiasm. She detailed her lessons in literature, where she delved into the worlds of Dickens and Twain, and her science classes, where she learned about the fascinating workings of the natural world. Her excitement was infectious, and even on the dreariest of days, Emma found herself looking forward to the postman's arrival with a new letter from Ada.

One day, as Emma sat reading one of Ada's letters aloud, Michael reached across the table and took her hand. "Emma, can I tell you how much your love has meant to me these past few months?" His voice was warm and sincere. "I don't know where I'd be without you in my life."

Emma looked up, her heart full. "Michael, you've become such a wonderful husband. And your love is helping me find peace with my past. I'm so grateful to be on this journey with you."

Michael squeezed her hand gently. "I'm honored to be your husband and friend, Emma. I see the strong, resilient, and compassionate woman that you are."

A sense of peace washed over her. "With that kind of support, I feel as though I can conquer anything. And Ada . . . she's thriving, too, isn't she?" She held up the letter she'd been reading. "I'm so glad we are able to connect with her through all these letters."

Michael smiled proudly. "Ada is a constant reminder of the beauty that can emerge from the ashes. We had such a rocky start to our family, and with Ada's illness, it sure wasn't the easiest time, was it?"

"No, but I'm so grateful that God brought us together and blessed us with this life we're building. You're an amazing father, Michael. Ada adores you, and so do I."

Michael leaned in to kiss her tenderly. "And I adore you, Emma. You are the light of my life, and I will spend every day showing you how deeply and completely you are loved."

Finally, she had begun to see herself through his eyes, recognizing her strength and worthiness in a new and healing way. She found safety in his unwavering love, and he became her rock, helping her rebuild her self-esteem. With time, even the memory of Samuel's betrayal lost its power over her.

One chilly afternoon in late November, Emma fretted about telling Ada their news. "When shall we tell her, Michael? Surely, she should know soon."

Michael pondered the question before answering. "I think we should tell her in person, dearest, when we see her in a few weeks."

As December's frost began to paint the windows of their lighthouse cottage, the air inside buzzed with a mix of anticipation and nervous energy. Emma sat by the fireplace one evening with a cup of tea, her insides churning with anxiety about the upcoming visit to Rochester where she would meet Michael's mother for the first time—and tell both she and Ada their news.

Michael took a seat beside her on the settee, near the crackling fire. "You've been rather quiet. Are you worried about meeting Mother?"

Emma looked up from her embroidery, her hands pausing as she met his concerned gaze. "A bit, yes." She tucked a loose strand of hair behind her ear. "I want to make a good impression. She means so much to you, and Ada adores her."

Michael smiled reassuringly and took her hand. "She'll adore you too. You know, she's quite excited to meet the woman who has captured my heart and been a wonderful mother to Ada."

"Really?" Emma's voice carried a hopeful note, but her heart still held a trace of worry.

"Yes, really." Michael chuckled, giving her hand a gentle squeeze. "Mother is very kind and open-hearted. She values family more than anything. Just be yourself, and she will see what I see."

Emma nodded, a bit relieved. "What's she like?"

Michael's eyes lit up. "She's spirited, full of life. Loves gardening. You should see her roses—they're the envy of the neighborhood. And though she's had an employee doing most of the cooking these days, she's an excellent cook. Her Christmas pudding is something of a legend in our family."

"That sounds lovely." Emma smiled, imagining the cozy scenes he described. "I think I'll bring one of my quilts as a gift. Do you think she'd like that?"

"Absolutely. She appreciates handmade gifts. She says they carry the warmth of the giver."

Their conversation drifted to plans for the holiday, discussing the journey to Rochester, the festive activities they might engage in, and the joy of being reunited with Ada. Emma's nerves began to settle as they planned, replaced by a growing excitement to experience the family holiday, to see Ada again, and to meet the matriarch who had shaped much of the man she loved.

And to tell them the news.

On Christmas morning, Michael awoke with a sense of jubilation that permeated the chilly air of his mother's home. The house was filled with the rich, comforting scents of pine from the Christmas tree and the subtle hints of cinnamon and nutmeg drifting from the kitchen. As he dressed in his Sunday best, a mixture of excite-ment and contentment settled over him, knowing that this Christmas was special. It was Emma's first holiday with his family, and he was reunited with Ada.

Descending the stairs, Michael found Emma and Ada already in the sitting room, exchanging laughter and stories by the glow of the fireplace. Emma, dressed elegantly in a deep green gown which complemented the festive decorations, turned to him with a smile that warmed him more than any fire could.

"Good morning, Michael. Merry Christmas!" Her eyes sparkled with holiday cheer.

"Merry Christmas, darling." He kissed her cheek softly before turning to Ada, who ran into his embrace. She was taller and even more willowy, but she'd gained a few needed pounds.

"Did you see what Santa brought me, Papa?" Ada's youthful excitement was infectious as she showed him an elaborate art set with pencils, paper, paint and brushes.

"I see that! Santa knows you well, my dear." His heart swelled with joy at the sight of his wife and daughter so happy.

"Good morning, family. Merry Christmas." His mother descended the stairs in a navy dress embellished with a long string of pearls.

The three of them echoed her greetings, almost in unison. After a simple breakfast of tea and warm scones, clotted cream, and raspberry jam, they walked to his mother's church, the streets blanketed in a layer of fresh snow that crunched under their feet.

The service was a heartwarming affair, filled with carols that echoed majestically through the decorated hall. Emma and his mother, seated side by side, shared hymnals and smiles, the initial awkwardness dissolved into a genuine affection that made him grateful.

Upon returning home, they were greeted by the mouthwatering aromas of Christmas dinner, a feast prepared by his mother's cook. The dining table was a spectacular sight, laden with roast goose, herbed stuffing, crisp Yorkshire puddings, and an array of vegetables glistening with butter. At the center of the table sat a large plum pudding, its dark, rich color promising the delightful flavors of spiced fruit.

"Everything looks wonderful." When Emma complimented the cook, the buxom woman blushed at the praise.

"Thank you, ma'am. I do hope everything is to your liking." She turned to Ada. "I gave Midnight an extra bowl of milk and a handful of goose, which he ate right up. He's fine in my room while you are in residence, Mrs. Diepolder. Ada warned us of your allergies." She quickly bustled back to the kitchen to oversee the serving of the meal.

Ada glanced at Emma. "Thank you."

As they settled around the table, Michael's mother, a woman of strong but gentle presence, took a moment to express her gratitude. "I am so pleased to have us all together this Christmas. Emma, dear, you have brought a new light into our family, and seeing everyone together like this is the best gift I could have asked for."

Emma reached across the table, squeezing her mother-in-law's hand. "Thank you. I am so grateful to be here, to be part of this family."

The meal was a lively affair, filled with laughter, stories from the past year, and plans for the next. Michael, watching the interactions between Emma, Ada, and his mother, basked in a profound sense of joy.

He and Emma shared a glance that carried a secret they were both eager to reveal. The time had come.

With a subtle nod, Emma reached for two small packages beside her chair. Ada and his mother waited, their anticipation palpable.

"We have one more gift we'd like to share with both of you. This one is very close to our hearts." Emma's voice trembled slightly.

Ada's eyes widened, and his mother leaned forward. Emma handed the first gift to Ada and the second to his mother. "Open them together, please."

They did as she bid, each holding up a tiny pair of beautifully crocheted baby booties, soft and pale green. Their eyes held confusion for a moment, but then his mother's twinkled with delight.

Ada's brow furrowed. "But I didn't get a baby doll this year."

He chuckled. "Actually, it's for someone who will be joining our family soon. You're going to be a big sister, Ada."

Ada's mouth dropped open, her fingers caressing the booties as the meaning sank in.

His mother guffawed. "And I'm going to be a grandmother again! How delightful!"

Emma smiled. "We wanted to share this with you on Christmas because it's a time of family, love, and new beginnings. He—or she—is due in the spring."

He grinned so wide, it almost hurt. "We'll call him 'Lawrence' or 'Laurie' if she's a girl."

"Really?" Ada burst out with joy—and with her usual flurry of questions. "This is wonderful! Can I make her something? Will he like stories? Can I teach him to draw?"

Emma laughed. "Yes, I know you'll make a wonderful big sister, and you'll teach him so many things, I'm sure."

His mother held up the booties, gazing at Emma tenderly. "You are truly a blessing to this family, Emma. I couldn't be happier about this news."

As the day drew to a close with cups of mulled wine and slices of Christmas pudding, gratitude for the love and warmth that filled his life nearly overwhelmed Michael. It was a Christmas that would be etched in his memory forever, a celebration of fresh beginnings and cherished traditions.

And new life.

About the Author

Susan G Mathis is an international award-winning, multi-published author of stories set in the beautiful Thousand Islands, her childhood stomping ground in upstate NY. Susan has been published more than thirty times in full-length novels, novellas, and non-fiction books. She has fourteen in her fiction line including, *The Fabric of Hope: An Irish Family Legacy*, *Christmas Charity*, *Katelyn's Choice*, *Devyn's Dilemma*, *Sara's Surprise*, *Reagan's Reward*, *Colleen's Confession*, *Peyton's Promise*, *Rachel's Reunion*, *Mary's Moment*, *A Summer at Thousand Island House*, *Libby's Lighthouse*, *Julia's Joy*, and *Emma's Engagement*. Her book awards include three Illumination Book Awards, four American Fiction Awards, three Indie Excellence Book Awards, five Literary Titan Book Awards, two Golden Scroll Awards, a Living Now Book Award, and a Selah Award.

Before Susan jumped into the fiction world, she served as the Founding Editor of *Thriving Family* magazine and the former Editor/Editorial Director of twelve Focus on the Family publications. Her first two published books were nonfiction. *Countdown for Couples: Preparing for the Adventure of Marriage* with an Indonesian and

Spanish version, and *The ReMarriage Adventure: Preparing for a Life of Love and Happiness*, have helped thousands of couples prepare for marriage. Susan is also the author of two picture books, *Lexie's Adventure in Kenya* and *Princess Madison's Rainbow Adventure*. Moreover, she is published in various book compilations including five *Chicken Soup for the Soul* books, *Ready to Wed*, *Supporting Families Through Meaningful Ministry*, *The Christian Leadership Experience*, and *Spiritual Mentoring of Teens*. Susan has also written several hundred published magazine and newsletter articles.

Susan is past president of American Christian Fiction Writers-CS (ACFW), former vice president of Christian Authors Network (CAN), a member of Christian Independent Publishing Association (CIPA), and a regular writer's contest judge. For over twenty years, Susan has been a speaker at writers' conferences, teachers' conventions, writing groups, and other organizational gatherings. Susan makes her home in Northern Virginia and enjoys traveling around the world but returns each summer to the Thousand Islands she loves. Visit www.SusanGMathis.com for more.

Acknowledgments

A special thanks...

To Judy Keeler, my wonderful historical editor, who combs through my manuscripts for accuracy. Because of her, you can trust that my stories are historically correct. And to Peter Hopper at Rock Island Lighthouse, who made sure the lighthouse information was accurate.

To my wonderful beta team, Judy, Laurie, Donna, Barb, Melinda, and Davalynn, who inspire me with your kindness, faithfulness, and wisdom. Thanks for all your hard work and wise input.

To my amazing publisher, Misty Beller, and rock-star editor, Denise Weimer. Thanks to you, I'm soaring on the wings of my writing journey.

And to all my dear friends who have journeyed with me in my writing. Thanks for your emails, social media posts, and especially for your reviews. Most of all, thanks for your friendship.

And to God, from whom all good gifts come. Without You, there would never be a dream or the ability to fulfill that dream. Thank You!

Author's Note

I hope you enjoyed *Emma's Engagement*. If you've read any of my other books, you know that I love introducing history to my readers through fictional stories. I hope this story sparks interest in our amazing past, especially the fascinating past of the marvelous Thousand Islands.

Rock Island Lighthouse and the Diepolder family are real, though some of the story is fashioned in my imagination, such as the scarlet fever episode. Please note that some of the timing is a little different than the historic record as I took a bit of creative license in bringing this story to life.

This is the last of three lighthouse stories, and I hope you'll enjoy them all. In the series, you'll meet the Row family women—Libby, Julia, and Emma—as they navigate the isolation, danger, and hope for lasting love at three different St. Lawrence River lighthouses. In book one, *Libby's Lighthouse*, you'll meet Libby and enjoy life at Tibbetts Lighthouse, and in book two, *Julia's Joy*, you'll experience life at Sister Island Lighthouse. Check out all fourteen of my Thousand Island stories at www.SusanGMathis.com/fiction.

Center Point Large Print
600 Brooks Road / PO Box 1
Thorndike, ME 04986-0001 USA

(207) 568-3717

US & Canada:
1 800 929-9108
www.centerpointlargeprint.com